"I'm sorry," he said s **pulling her into his arms.**

For a moment, she stood there stiffly...but then she collapsed against him. Not to cry, just because she *needed* his strength and solid body. She flung her arms around his waist and held on for dear life. That had to be his cheek resting on her head. His chest rumbled with words she didn't even try to make out. This felt like more than reassurance.

Jordan kept clinging even as awareness of him as a man, not a friend, stirred in her. His powerful thighs pressed hers, and her breasts were flattened on his broad, muscular chest.

She couldn't let him see what she was feeling. She didn't dare *feel* any of this. But when she finally summoned the will to step away, that involved lifting her head and looking at him.

His gaze flicked down to her mouth, and she knew: he was thinking about kissing her.

And right this second, there was nothing in the world she wanted more than that.

BLACK WIDOW

USA TODAY BESTSELLING AUTHOR
JANICE KAY JOHNSON

INTRIGUE

Harlequin®
INTRIGUE™

Recycling programs for this product may not exist in your area.

ISBN-13: 978-1-335-45701-1

Black Widow

Copyright © 2024 by Janice Kay Johnson

Harlequin Enterprises ULC
22 Adelaide St. West, 41st Floor
Toronto, Ontario M5H 4E3, Canada
www.Harlequin.com

Printed in Lithuania

MIX
Paper | Supporting responsible forestry
FSC® C021394

CAST OF CHARACTERS

Jordan Hendrick—Years after she escaped her hometown of Storm Lake because of a rush to judgment, Jordan must face the past. Suspicion over the murders of two men she'd briefly dated follows her home.

Shelly Hendrick—Shelly has supported Jordan's choices...and her innocence. Her debilitating stroke is the catalyst that brings Jordan within easy reach of the family that hates her and the community that judges her.

Tom Moore—Rehabilitating after a shoot-out, Detective Tom Moore accepts a job in a quiet community. He dislikes the undercover role he's persuaded to take on: a friendly neighbor who is really staking out the notorious Jordan Hendrick. He knows better than to fall for a woman who will detest him once she knows who he really is.

Steve Dunn—Storm Lake's golden boy and football star, Steve responded to life's disappointments with violent outbursts. Could the people who'd adored him ever believe he had a dark side?

Kevin Dunn—Having worshipped his big brother, Kevin knows who to blame for Steve's downfall.

Ronald Bowen—Steve's uncle, now Storm Lake deputy police chief, shares the family opinion, although his long career in law enforcement gives him a moderating perspective. Or does it?

An author of more than ninety books for children and adults with more than seventy-five for Harlequin, **Janice Kay Johnson** writes about love and family and pens books of gripping romantic suspense. A *USA TODAY* bestselling author and an eight-time finalist for the Romance Writers of America RITA® Award, she won a RITA® Award in 2008. A former librarian, Janice raised two daughters in a small town north of Seattle, Washington.

Books by Janice Kay Johnson

Harlequin Intrigue

Visit the Author Profile page at Harlequin.com.

Prologue

The front door slammed. She straightened, the muscles between her shoulders knotting as her husband stomped toward the kitchen with a heavy tread that roused fear she hadn't felt in a while. They'd been doing so well! He'd been especially unhappy at work recently, though, and if his supervisor so much as mentioned he'd been impolite to a customer, it would have festered all day. If he'd been fired…

The pie! After grabbing pot holders, she hastily took it from the oven, shoving the door shut with one foot. He'd be happy that she'd baked it for him, wouldn't he?

A solidly built man who towered a foot over her average height, his hands were already tightened into fists when he came in sight and a dark scowl made his face ugly. "What's that?"

"It's…it's a raspberry pie." Hating herself for feeling timid, she held it out even though it was too hot for him to take into his hands. "Raspberries are just coming ripe. When I saw them, I thought about you—"

He advanced on her, menace in his body language. "Where did you see them?"

She retreated until her back came up against the kitchen table. "I…had lunch with Mom. We stopped at the farmers' market after."

"Who were you meeting?" snarled the man she had once

believed she loved and had been trying to convince herself she could love again.

"What?" Her tongue tangled. "I don't know what you're talking about!"

"Then why didn't you tell me you were seeing your mother today?"

He was so close now, she felt his spittle on her cheeks. Her hands shook. If she didn't set this pie down... "She called this morning—I didn't think—"

"You thought wrong!" he bellowed, fist already swinging. Connecting with her right cheekbone.

Crying out, she staggered and dropped the pie. The ceramic dish shattered at her feet, splattering its hot contents on her legs and his. As she cowered, she couldn't tell if her blurred vision was from the blow or from tears.

"You promised!" she cried. He'd *sobbed* when he apologized and swore he'd never hurt her again.

"You know the rules." His next blow struck her shoulder as she turned away to protect herself. "You tell me if you have to leave the house *before* you leave it."

She fell to her knees and then hands, which slid in the berry filling. Blood. It looked like blood.

He kicked her in the belly before she could curl into a ball to protect herself.

"No!" she cried. "I was trying to do something nice for you!"

"You think I'm a fool?" The blows kept coming.

After the time when she thought she might die, almost six months ago, she'd sworn that she wouldn't submit to this again. Now, fear awakened anger. She wouldn't be his punching bag because something had gone wrong today.

Even knowing it to be useless, she thrashed, kicking her feet out at him.

His booted foot slammed into her, over and over, as if her ineffectual struggles only enraged him more. Terrified, she looked up to see his gun in his hand. He always carried it somewhere on him. Nobody was going to tell him he couldn't. Not even his boss.

Now, it was aimed right at her, and she saw death in his eyes.

He was supposed to love her. And now…was it too late to stop him?

No. Somehow, she calculated distance and angle. Sliding to her back, she slammed both feet up as hard as she could, with such effort her butt left the kitchen floor. Those feet struck him right where it hurt him most.

On a guttural cry, he clutched himself, letting the gun slip out of his hand. It fell into the mess from the dropped pie. This was her only chance.

She flung herself forward and got her hand on that gun. He bragged about having one of those cop pieces with no safety, so she didn't have to think whether it was locked or not and take a chance of getting it wrong.

"You bitch!" he screamed, and followed that up with a string of the worst obscenities she'd ever heard. "I'm going to kill you. I swear I am."

Despite his pain, he kicked her head. Ears ringing, she slid a few feet, but still managed to lift the gun and point it at him. Trying to scrabble away gained her mere inches. Pain splintered through her head.

Through chattering teeth, she cried, "Leave me alone— Let me go, or I swear…"

He threw his big muscular body at her.

She pulled the trigger. Once, twice…and he crashed down on her. Her head hit the floor, and the whole world went black.

Chapter One

Jordan Hendrick stared up at the night sky, rapt, as impossibly golden fireworks melted while drifting in twinkling sparks toward the ground before vanishing. Her butt was sore, because she was sitting on a blanket spread over a rock-hard mowed soccer field, but that was a small price to pay for the fun of joining the townspeople to watch a really spectacular fireworks show. And she hadn't come with a casual group of friends this time, either; no, she was on a real date.

The music playing from giant speakers reached a crescendo, and a dozen fireworks at a time exploded into the sky in the grand finale. Everyone oohed and aahed, including her. The wonder on the face of a young girl sitting near Jordan was almost as entrancing as the fireworks. Jordan's heart melted just a little, but for some reason the sight of such open, uncomplicated joy also triggered a pang of sadness. When had she last let herself feel anything like that?

Unfortunately, she knew. She hadn't been that much older than the girl when she'd last been able to trust life to be full of possibilities.

As the display ended, she shook herself. All around her, people started gathering themselves and their possessions. The man she'd been sharing the blanket with did the same, and she stood to help him shake it out and fold it. A minute later, he held out his hand for hers so they could join the crowd clumped and waiting turns to mill through one of the handful of gates in the chain-link fence surrounding the field.

Being on a date at all felt surreal to Jordan, even though this was actually the second time she'd gone out with Elliott Keefe. He was a real estate agent at a Walla Walla Windermere office, where she dropped off mail daily. Pleasant chats had become a mild flirtation, and she'd astounded herself by agreeing to dinner last weekend at a highly rated restaurant that specialized in the local wines this area in eastern Washington was known for. Then came the picnic and fireworks for the Fourth of July this week. Nice as it was—he smiled at her just then and squeezed her hand— Jordan already knew this wouldn't go anywhere. For her, though, this was a venture into the strange new world of pretending she had something in common with her peers.

She was twenty-eight years old, and this was only the second guy she'd gone out with in the past eight years.

A whisper in her left ear that she couldn't quite make out had her turning, off guard when a moment later, a shoulder bumped her, hard. She stumbled and would have gone down if Elliott hadn't caught her. He glared, but from the way his head turned it was apparent he couldn't tell who'd been so determined to get ahead. By the time they reached the gate, she'd been jostled a couple more times, but the lighting wasn't good and anyone who bumped her could just as well have been pushed from behind themselves.

Or so she told herself. This past week, she'd felt uneasy, off and on, as if someone was watching her. The past couple of years, she'd had three distinct periods with the same creepy feeling that lingered for a few days, but nothing had come of it. Something was different this time, though:

Wednesday she'd have sworn someone had been in her half of a duplex, and *that* was new.

Except…it was all in her mind. It had to be. She hadn't actually *seen* anyone staring at her or following her, and just because her butcher knife lay out on her clean kitchen counter where she'd never have left it wasn't enough to call 911…and tell them what to investigate?

Ignoring that twinge she sometimes got between her shoulder blades, the one that whispered, *look around*, she gripped Elliott's hand and focused on keeping to her feet as they hustled in front of cars inching toward the exits from the lot. The headlights were too blinding for her to make out faces around her, anyway.

"I had a good time," Elliott said just then.

"Me, too." Jordan didn't protest when he wrapped an arm around her shoulders and steered her toward her car. She liked the warmth of his embrace as long as he kept it loose like this, but was also a tiny bit glad she'd insisted on driving herself.

"I wish I'd been able to pick you up," he grumbled mildly, "but it's not as if I won't see you sometime this week."

"Unless you're out showing houses when I drop by," she teased. "Which you should hope you will be."

"I do have some great listings right now."

Her diversion had worked, and his enthusiasm sparked. He kept talking, stopping only when they reached her car, and she unlocked it.

This kiss was more serious than the one last weekend, but not a lot. More…warm and pleasant. A coworker of hers who liked to talk about the constantly changing roster of men in her life would have said, *meh*. Jordan knew that in this case, it was likely because of her, not anything wrong with him. Given her history, letting herself relax enough to enjoy any kind of intimacy with a man might never be possible. They said their good-nights, and once behind the wheel of her car, she worked her way into the slow traffic dissipating onto the city streets.

At least she'd found the courage to *try* to start something with a man again. Even baby steps were something to celebrate, Jordan decided twenty minutes later, as she let herself in her front door.

JORDAN DIDN'T HAPPEN to see Elliott the next day when she dashed into Windermere with a pile of mail bundled with a rubber band. Some days she left it in their box at the street, but today the batch had been too bulky. The cheerful woman at the front desk looked up with a smile. "I haven't seen Elliott yet today."

Jordan flipped a friendly hand at her just before the glass door closed behind her and she trotted toward her postal vehicle. It was out of character for her to have ever taken the time to talk to the good-looking guy who'd shown an interest in her. Truthfully, she hustled all day.

Mail delivery looked a lot easier than it was. Her first day on the job, her grumpy supervisor had had to wait for her, the last person by over an hour to make it back into the office. But now that she was on her fourth year, she'd long since learned the tricks to allow her to move fast.

Even now, though, she hadn't gotten over being exhausted by the time she carried her empty trays into the back of the post office at the end of the day, sorted what mail had appeared in the interim to give herself a jump start in the morning, and clocked out.

Maybe she'd settle for a salad tonight. Or something out of the freezer. She was happier in her solitude than a young woman her age should be, but she had several episodes of a show she was streaming to watch and was eager to get back to it.

She hadn't gotten further than studying the contents of her freezer before her doorbell rang. Jordan jumped at the sound. Who on earth…?

She of all people didn't like surprises. She hadn't forgotten that the last guy she'd dated had been killed several years ago after surprising burglars in his house—or so the police believed. Violent crime happened everywhere, even in a nice town like Walla Walla, built around a high-end liberal arts college. Since there was no peephole in the door, she cracked the blinds to see a large, dark sedan in her driveway. It bristled with antennae, and the bumper didn't look like the one on *her* car.

Wary, she opened the door without removing the chain. A man and a woman stood on her small front porch. Both wore badges and holstered guns on their belts. Jordan had seen stern looks like that before.

"Ms. Hendrick?" the man said politely, but with no give in his voice. "I'm Detective Shannon and this is Detective Dutton. May we come in?"

Her fingers clenched on the door and her heart pounded in her ears. "May I ask what this is about?"

"It has to do with an attempted murder that took place last night. I believe you know the victim."

"Victim…" Her forehead creased. A coworker or— "Oh, God, not Elliott Keefe?"

"I'm afraid so." The words might sound sympathetic, but the expression on his face remained watchful.

No. How could that be?

She closed the door as her fingers fumbled with the chain to let the cops in. Not just cops—detectives. They had to be, didn't they, since they were plainclothes?

She evaluated them automatically. The man was bulky in the way of a former high school or college athlete, his hair graying at the temples. His wedding ring caught her eye. The woman had to be midthirties, lean like a runner. Her glance took in Jordan's small living room thoroughly before she met Jordan's eyes with a look that hadn't softened at all.

"Please, sit down." Jordan gestured at the sofa before her legs dropped her into the wooden rocking chair. "Can you tell me what happened? Is he badly injured?"

The man took the lead. "Mr. Keefe was found unconscious midday by a coworker who went to check on him. Apparently, he had appointments set up, but didn't come into work."

"He was…excited about some new listings." She almost continued, but of course they knew how real estate sales happened.

"A different coworker mentioned that the two of you were seeing each other. She said you're employed as a mail carrier."

With her hands twined together on her lap, Jordan's fingers tightened painfully. "Yes. Although seeing each other is putting it strongly. We've gone out twice, that's all. He's nice, but…"

Those implacable stares silenced her.

"When did you see him last?" the woman asked.

Jordan had no doubt that they already knew the answer to that question. Elliott had probably talked about his plans at work.

"Yesterday. Because it was the Fourth—" as if they didn't know about the national holiday "—he brought a picnic dinner, and we ate it at the soccer field before the fireworks started."

"And afterward?" Detective Dutton again.

"He walked me to my car, and we said good-night."

"Said good-night?"

Her cheeks heated. "He kissed me. It was brief because there were people all around."

"You had driven separately." The male cop—Jordan couldn't remember his name—picked up where his partner had left off.

"That's right. Even though it was a holiday, earlier in the day Elliott showed several houses to a couple who had trouble finding time. He offered to pick me up anyway, but…" She looked away for a moment, then made herself face them. "I preferred driving myself. I'm not in a hurry to take a casual relationship anywhere. It's easier if he doesn't see me to my doorstep at the end of the evening."

Something shifted on the woman's face that suggested she understood and had made the same choice in the past.

Jordan looked from one to the other. "You haven't said how he is now."

"I'm afraid he's in a coma." The woman cop spoke with surprising gentleness, given their attitude to that point. "We believe his assailant thought Mr. Keefe was dead. In fact, he's still in critical condition."

"Oh God." Jordan bent forward as if she had to protect herself. How could this be?

"Your name came up," the man said.

Of course it had. She waited with dread.

"Having to do with another man you were *seeing* at the time." The emphasis on *seeing* was unmistakable. "A Pete Shroder."

"He was killed during some kind of home invasion." Did she sound shrill? She took a slow breath to calm herself.

"Or at least, that's what I heard. That his house had been cleaned out, and he surprised them just before they left."

"That's true, but it's interesting that the physical assault on Mr. Keefe looks a good deal like the one on Mr. Shroder. A gunshot—two in Mr. Shroder's case—that probably brought each man down, followed by a brutal beating."

She had to face her peril straight on, even if she felt so nauseated she wanted to run for the bathroom. "And you think *I* could have had something to do with those attacks."

"I didn't say that," the man corrected her. "We're interested because of the fact that you had a relationship with both of them."

Mouth dry, she said, "Pete died three years ago. He and I went out only a couple of times, and I doubt either of us would have bothered to continue seeing each other. I hadn't seen him in several days before he was murdered." Jordan glared at them. "I don't see how you can have failed to find and arrest his killer by now."

Wooden expressions suggested she'd hit them where it hurt.

"Unfortunately, neither the bullet nor the trace evidence led us anywhere, suggesting the killer had not formerly been in trouble with the law."

Both raised their brows as they continued to look at *her.*

"You're wasting your time with me. I don't, and have never, owned a gun." She'd only fired one once in her life, and the memory so horrified her she shied away from it. "I'm law-abiding, polite and verging on timid. I rarely even date. I can't imagine any way these two attacks could have anything to do with me." She rose to her feet. "If you feel the need to come back with more implied accusations, I'll need to hire an attorney before I speak to you again."

A twitch in his face might have been a suppressed grimace. Both produced cards and handed them over.

"Thank you. Now, unless there's some other way I can help…?"

"Can you think of any other connection between these two men?"

"Only the obvious, which I trust you already know. Pete worked in property management, and very possibly crossed paths with Elliott." She swallowed. "Am I permitted to visit Elliott at the hospital?"

Detective Dutton—Beverly, according to the card—shook her head. "He's in the ICU. Only family is permitted in to see him, and even they're limited."

Jordan nodded, a sort of numbness creeping over her. Shock, of course.

Detective Shannon opened the door and held it for his partner, then turned back to Jordan. "I encourage you not to leave town."

She was still speechless when he closed the door behind him. A minute later, she heard the car out front drive away.

THE NEXT FEW days were agonizing. She couldn't stop thinking about Elliott—she called the hospital each evening to hear how he was doing, despite the fact that she was given only nonanswers.

The first time she had to take the mail into the real estate office, she said, "I heard about Elliott. It's so awful! You must all be shaken up."

Of course they were. At least no one looked at her as if it had occurred to them that she might have started knocking off men after she'd gone out with them a time or two.

She searched reviews online for a criminal attorney in the event she needed to hire one. The experience was new to her, even though she'd had one before. That time, her mother had decided who to hire while Jordan was still in the hospital.

However, she didn't hear a word from either detective in this case. The *Walla Walla Union-Bulletin* reported that police were investigating but had given no indication they were closing in on a suspect or suspects.

Friday when she handed over the mail at the Windermere office, the woman behind the counter beamed at her. "You probably already know Elliott has regained consciousness! It'll still be a few weeks before he can make it back to work, but that's such good news!"

A huge weight lifted off Jordan's shoulders. "Yes, it is."

"He's going to be mad that two of his listings have sold while he was in the hospital. He was so determined to be the selling *and* the listing agent on both of them."

"He talked about that." She hesitated. "I was told he couldn't have flowers in Intensive Care, but maybe I'll order some now."

"We're planning the same," she was assured.

Jordan felt wobbly with relief when she returned to her vehicle. For once, she didn't jog and leap in. Once behind the wheel, she just sat there for a minute. Nothing about the attack had been her fault, but still… Thank God. He was going to be all right.

A few days later, she received a stiff note thanking her for the bouquet—from Elliott's mother. Maybe he wasn't up to writing notes yet—but Jordan wondered. If one of the detectives had shared the *interesting* coincidence of her having dated two men who had almost immediately thereafter suffered similar attacks, wouldn't Elliott tell himself he'd be smart to stay away from her?

The continuing silence confirmed her guess. It stung,

even though he could just have sensed how tepid her interest in him was. He might well not have asked her out again no matter. She did her best to wedge mail into the Windermere box that she once would have carried in.

Jordan kept expecting to hear from the detectives again—they would surely have researched her background more thoroughly by now—but the call that came in just as she left the post office at the end of her shift, two weeks to the day after Elliott was attacked, didn't come from the local area code. She knew this one, though; she'd grown up in Storm Lake, Idaho. Only...she didn't recognize the number. It wasn't her mother's or one belonging to any of the few other people she'd stayed in touch with.

"Hello?" she said cautiously.

A woman said, "Is this Jordan Hendrick?"

"Yes, it is."

"I'm calling from Cavanaugh Memorial Hospital in Storm Lake," she said kindly. "I'm sorry to have to tell you that your mother has had a stroke."

Chapter Two

Mom is alive. Jordan had at least that much to cling to. Some of the rest of what the hospital representative had said wasn't as encouraging. The ER doctor had done everything he could for her, but Mom hadn't been found as quickly as would have been ideal, so there were noticeable and disturbing effects that, she was assured, would improve with physical therapy.

Jordan had no idea who had found Mom. Was it like Elliott, that she hadn't shown up at her job in the city auditor's office? Maybe. Probably. Although Mom had more friends than Jordan did. Any of them could have been concerned if Mom didn't call when she'd promised, or missed a garden club meeting.

Oh, she hated thinking of her mother collapsed on the floor, unable to grasp her phone or, if she had succeeded, make herself understood. Had she tried to crawl?

Jordan shuddered.

She didn't remember the drive back to the duplex, only flying in her front door. All she could think was to pack as fast as she could. Most of the furniture had come with the place; the rest, she'd abandon. Mom would need her for a long time. She couldn't let herself think that Mom wouldn't because... No!

Jordan didn't have enough boxes to contain her books, so she carried piles of them out and set them loose in the trunk of her car. Clothes and shoes, first in her suitcases, then in white plastic trash bags.

Coat closet. Couldn't forget that.

The doorbell rang and she jumped six inches. What now?

Mostly uncaring, she flung open her door. Of course it had to be the pair of detectives on her porch again, expressions unchanged from the last visit. She knew why they were back, but right now she didn't *care*.

Both of their gazes went past her and fixed on the suitcases sitting by the front door. That couldn't be a surprise, since they had parked at the curb this time, and walked past her car with the trunk and one door standing open, many of her possessions already loaded.

Detective Shannon raised an eyebrow. "Going somewhere?"

"Yes." She backed up. "You can come in, but whatever you plan to say, you have to make it quick."

The detective stepped inside, followed by his partner. "Hoping to get out of town before we came back to talk to you?" he asked sardonically. "Or did you forget I asked you to stay available?"

"I would have called." Her eyes burned from the tears she'd refused to shed. "My mother had a stroke. I'm going home."

"That would be Storm Lake in Idaho."

"Yes. Mom's in the hospital. It was a serious stroke. If—*when*—she makes it home, I need to be there to take care of her."

"Interesting timing."

Interesting had become one of her least favorite words.

"It's horrible timing. I've been sick about Elliott, and now this."

"Please sit down," he suggested. "You have a long drive ahead of you. I guess you're not planning to fly."

Jordan shook her head. "That would be so complicated, it would take longer than driving." And she'd have to leave way more behind, or figure out how to ship it, or…

"Well, then, ten or fifteen minutes isn't going to make any difference."

Of course it could! But she was law-abiding, and she understood why they had more questions. So she sat, even as she quivered with the need to leap up and keep packing, to get on the road.

"We found your fingerprints on file in Idaho."

"If you'd asked, I'd have told you they are. I know what you discovered, but there was never any suggestion that I was at fault for what happened. It was clearly self-defense. I was in the hospital for days after the…incident." Oh, why be squeamish? But she couldn't make herself be blunt.

"You're right," he conceded.

His partner hadn't said a word, but she was listening. Her gaze was trained on Jordan's face, too, reading the range of emotions that must be crowding each other.

"That said, it's hard to believe it's chance that you would have been involved in another man's death. That you fired the shot that killed him."

She shuddered and resented the vulnerability he'd exposed. "He would have killed me if I hadn't pulled that trigger."

"That seems to be the consensus," he agreed.

She bounced to her feet. "Please. I need to go. You didn't find my fingerprints or anything else pointing to me at either Pete Shroder's house or Elliott's because I'd never been to either one. There's nothing more I can tell you. You can call me anytime. I'll answer unless I'm in the hospital."

Detective Dutton touched her partner's arm. Only a brief contact, but he gave her a surprised glance. Then his mouth tightened, and he grudgingly stood.

"Very well. At this point, I can't compel you to stay in Walla Walla. Please get in touch with us if you think of anything that might be helpful. We'd appreciate it."

He'd think she was making up stories if she told him about feeling watched, about the whisper in her ear that she hadn't made out just before someone buffeted her, about the knife left out on her kitchen counter. A knife she hadn't used in days.

But even if they didn't doubt her credibility, none of that had anything to do with an attempt to kill Elliott. Jordan didn't see how it possibly could.

So she nodded, thanked them when they carried her suitcases and a couple of bags out to her car, and got a tiny bit teary when stern Detective Shannon paused after opening the driver's side door of the unmarked car, looked at her over the roof, and said, "Drive carefully, Ms. Hendrick. You're shaken right now. You need to focus on the road." He sounded positively human.

She smiled shakily at him. "I'll do that. I've driven this route plenty of times."

He dipped his head and climbed in. A moment later, the unmarked police car drove away.

Kitchen. She couldn't leave food to spoil. Jordan hurried back into the duplex, making lists in her head of all the people she had to call, and everything that remained for her to do before she left.

Given the difficulty of her mother's recovery, Jordan

knew she'd be committed in Storm Lake too long to ever take up her job again or move back into this duplex.

THE FIRST THING San Francisco PD Homicide Detective Tom Moore knew was pain. The second was recognition of one of his least favorite locations: the hospital. He didn't even have to open his eyes to know where he was. The beeps of life-sustaining machines and the smells were all he needed.

Those beeps sounded close, as if it might be *his* life the machines were sustaining. Given the extremity of his pain, that seemed possible.

A firm voice spoke in his ear, and he flinched. He immediately regretted even that tiny motion.

"Detective Moore. Are you back with us?"

Where else would he have been?

He grunted.

"We're preparing to take you into surgery. I don't know if you recall what happened to you…"

He hadn't gotten that far yet, but now he did. Approaching a house with his partner to speak to a witness to a murder who was possibly a suspect. Reaching for his sidearm when the front door was thrust open unexpectedly. Max yelling a warning Tom hadn't needed even before gunfire erupted. Reeling as the first bullet struck him, losing some touch with reality as he felt as if a horde of yellow jackets were stinging him. Falling, falling, his nerveless hand losing touch with the grip of his Sig Sauer. That hand flopping on top of a dandelion. Strange that was the last thing he saw.

"Max," he mumbled.

"What?"

"Max." His mouth felt like sandpaper. "Partner."

"Oh." The pause stretched painfully long. "I'm sorry. Detective Cortez didn't make it."

Tom hadn't realized he'd opened his eyes until they fell shut. He couldn't have said what the woman looked like, except she wore one of those starched white uniforms.

"My fault," he managed to say.

Her hand touched his forehead like a benediction. "I very much doubt that," she murmured.

A bright light hung overhead. Somebody else started talking to him as they lifted his arm. Must be time... Yeah.

MACHINES BEEPED, although Mom was breathing on her own.

Jordan had stayed at her mother's bedside as much as hospital personnel allowed. The chair was comfortable enough that, with the addition of a pillow and a blanket, she could nap for stretches. She found her way at intervals to the cafeteria drawn by the smell of coffee, her feet knowing the way. Life had a surreal quality. Most of her breaks happened when one or the other of her mother's friends came by to check on her, or even asked for a turn to sit with her.

Mom's face was twisted enough to make her appear almost a stranger. Jordan wondered whether her mother's friends found that as disturbing as she did. The hand Jordan held so often was a claw; with the IV on Mom's other side, the chair had been placed so that visitors didn't get in the way of nurses and doctors coming and going.

Worst of all was when Mom tried to speak, and all that came out was a garbled mockery of her voice. She couldn't speak a coherent word.

Jordan swore Mom recognized her. Her eyes—one only partially open—stayed fixed on Jordan's face whenever she was in the room and Mom wasn't sleeping.

"I think she looks better," Bonnie Feller insisted as they met in the waiting room. A plump, attractive woman who was allowing a streak of gray to appear in her dark hair, she'd arrived for today's visit shortly after Jordan was banned from the room while Mom underwent physical therapy. Jordan couldn't imagine what that consisted of.

"You really think so?" she asked doubtfully.

"I do," Bonnie assured her. "She couldn't lie on her back at first, only curled on her side in this almost—"

Fetal position. That's what she'd been about to say.

Jordan nodded. It was true.

Hurrying to change the subject, Bonnie patted her on the hand. "Guy was so glad to hear that you're home again. I'm sure he'll call you one of these days."

Uh-huh. Sure he would. Personally, Jordan would rather hear from Detective Shannon.

Bonnie and Mom had been friends since Jordan's family moved to Storm Lake when she'd been a toddler. Bonnie's son Guy was a year older than Jordan. Apparently the two of them had happily been playmates into the early years of elementary school, when he'd dug in his heels one day and said, "She's a *girl*!" He'd been forced to attend one more of her birthday parties, but had been so appalled that he was the only boy, his mother gave up thereafter. By high school, they were casually friendly, but never having even a hint of romantic feelings. Back then, Jordan would have said they regarded each other almost as siblings.

Guy had been away at the University of Idaho during the years of Jordan's marriage. After a summer home, he'd left for Washington State University for a graduate degree in veterinary science. Jordan saw him a couple of times that summer, and wished she hadn't.

Mom, who kept her updated on everyone she'd known, had reported that a couple of years ago he'd bought into the only small animal practice right here in town. That knowledge would be enough to keep her from adopting a dog or cat. For all the years she and Guy had known each other, he'd been one of the many people who'd had doubt, and more, in their eyes when they'd looked at her that summer.

Did you really have *to kill your husband?*

How could Guy not have known her better than that? But then, he'd played on the football team with Steve Dunn, taken classes with him, gone to the same keggers. For all that Guy was in an accelerated academic program, he mostly hung out with his jock friends. Jordan had been to those same parties as Steve's girlfriend, awed by his swagger and charisma even as she hovered unobtrusively to one side, sipping at a single beer as long as she could make it last. Astonished at her luck, wondering what the homecoming king and star football player with Steve's looks had possibly seen in *her*.

Well, she soon learned. He'd seen a vulnerability she didn't know lurked deep inside her. Having her father walk out and never bother with her again did damage that she hadn't really understood. Steve? He'd seen that he could dominate and terrorize her, and thought she'd never fight back.

He'd almost been right.

She could ignore people like Guy Feller. Mom had always been there for her when Jordan would allow it, and she had every intention of doing anything and everything she could to get her mother back on her feet, able to deadhead the roses in her garden, have lunch with friends like Bonnie and flirt with Mr. Enyart, who owned the plant nursery. Most of her contemporaries in this town could go to hell, though, as far as she was concerned.

The nurse appeared and beamed at Jordan. "You're welcome to come back again!"

Jordan smiled at her mother's friend. "Why don't you go first?" Only one person was permitted at a time. "I might wander out in the courtyard and see if there's still a sun in the sky."

Bonnie laughed and rose to her feet, clutching her handbag. "You take your time, dear. You know your mother wouldn't want you to exhaust yourself the way you have been."

"Thank you, Bonnie."

Watching her hurry away behind the nurse, Jordan slouched deeper in the waiting room chair. The sun would feel nice—but another cup of coffee might do her more good.

TWO DAYS LATER, more tired than ever, Jordan parked in the driveway—Mom's car occupied the single-vehicle detached garage—detoured to grab the mail from the box out at the street, and was flipping through it as she trudged back to the house. Not much today, thank goodness—mostly advertising flyers and a couple of what appeared to be getwell cards from people whose names Jordan recognized. Not until she glanced up as she put her foot on the first step did she see a bobbing movement right in front of her. She started, then realized a helium balloon was tied to the doorknob.

Several white gravestones featuring skulls-and-crossbones stood out on the black balloon. Standard Halloween fare, she thought, in the distant way one did at a moment like this. It was the bloodred words scrawled below the stones that chilled her.

Large letters spelled out *Welcome Home,* while smaller letters beneath added, *Where You Belong.*

Was someone watching, enjoying her reaction?

She spun on her heels but saw no one. Which didn't mean someone wasn't out there.

If she hadn't been so tired, the message might not have hit her so hard. As it was, hurt warred with rage. Rage won. Let whoever had done this *see* what she felt!

She already had her keys in her hand. She leaped up the steps and used the car key to stab the damn balloon. She wanted to keep stabbing, but it deflated fast with a hiss. All she could do was tear the ribbon from the doorknob and take the thing into the kitchen.

There, feeling vengeful, she cut it into shreds with scissors, wishing she could send them to whatever creep had been so determined to remind her of those shattering moments when she had to choose her own life or Steve's. Then she buried them—unfortunate pun—under some messy vegetable trimmings in the trash can.

Finally, she sat at the kitchen table, hands shaking, teeth chattering, and asked herself, *Why?* And, *Was this a threat, or only a needle jab to remind her what a terrible person she must be?*

Only belatedly did she wish she'd photographed the balloon before she destroyed it.

TOM ALMOST DIDN'T recognize the woman who stepped into his room at the rehab center, where he'd been moved after a ten-day stay at the hospital. Emilia Cortez looked as if she'd lost more weight than should be possible so quickly, her eyes were red-rimmed, and her skin no longer had that usual glow. Max had worshipped his pretty wife and been thrilled when she gave birth to the world's cutest baby girl six months ago. It would never have occurred to him that he'd be killed on the job. For all the drama injected in thrillers, movies and TV shows, detectives were far less at risk than front-line patrol officers.

She shuffled like an old woman to his bedside. "Oh, Tom." Her failing attempt at a smile told him how bad he looked.

Damn it, he was going to cry now. "Emilia, I'm so sorry. I should have guessed we were walking into a disaster. Max was depending on me."

She perched on the edge of the bed, tiny enough to barely depress the mattress. "No, you two worked together. Don't lie to me. He had no more idea than you did."

That was true, but—

"He shot that monster, you know." Actually, *monster* wasn't her choice of word; she used a deeply angry word in Spanish that Tom hadn't known until he paired with Maximo Cortez and expanded his own vocabulary. None of which he'd have expected to hear from this sweet woman. "At least he's dead."

"Yeah." He reached out for her hand. "Max saved my life." Another bullet or two hitting him, or even just a delay in getting him to the hospital, and he wouldn't be here now. "I wish it was the other way around." His throat felt clogged and his eyes burned.

"He would be glad. That's what I came to say. You were Max's best friend, not just his partner. If he'd had to choose—" This time, her voice broke.

"He should have chosen himself," he said harshly. "He had you and Lidia to think of. I don't have a wife or children. I wouldn't be missed the same way."

She tilted her head and studied him for longer than felt comfortable. "You've been given a chance to have all that. That's what I came to say. Live gladly, Tom."

His throat all but closed up.

"For now, Lidia and I are going to stay with Max's mama. She needs us, and it will be good for Lidia to have her *abuela*, too."

"Yes." He tightened his fingers on hers. "If you ever need me—"

She kissed his cheek lightly. "I'll always know you would come if I called, but...I have family."

He didn't, something he rarely regretted, but this was one of those moments. He had friends, sure, but they had lives and families of their own. He couldn't exactly go knocking and say, "Hey, can I move in for a few months? Just until I can walk and maybe grip a gun and even squeeze a trigger?"

No.

But lucky him. Barely ten minutes after Emilia had left him to a grim mood, a light rap on the door presaged the upbeat voice he'd come to dread: his physical therapist.

Tom had never backed off from a challenge before, though, and wasn't about to start this time. Whatever it took to regain strength in his damaged body, he'd do. So far, he tried to avoid facing the truth that returning to the peak physical conditioning required for his job with the police department in a major urban city was a long way off, if possible at all.

They had already let him know he could go on desk duty, which held zero appeal. Maybe he'd find a...transitional job. Yeah, that was it. Probably not for a couple of months yet, if not longer, but he'd bet there were smaller towns out there who'd hire him because of his experience, understanding he might not be prepared to run down a suspect and tackle him the first day of his new employment.

And maybe he'd be investigating the theft of equipment from a rental business, minor embezzling, a holdup at the tavern. Considering his goal had always been to work homicide, that didn't stir a lot of excitement, but it would beat shuffling paper and answering phones. When he was ready, he had no doubt SFPD would reinstate him after his time away to heal.

Growling under his breath as he laboriously transferred himself to the wheelchair, he thought, *Make it a small town on flat ground.*

Chapter Three

"You...gave...up..." Mom swallowed hard before she was able to continue working to shape her mouth and control her tongue to make her speech legible. "So...much."

Having no trouble understanding her anymore, Jordan smiled and gave her a side hug. "Don't be silly. I'm taking a long vacation because I don't have to pay any rent. My job wasn't very exciting, you know. I'd made friends, but none close enough for me to be likely to stay in touch. I've missed you so much. You gave me the excuse I needed to come home. I just wish it wasn't such a traumatic one for you."

They sat in the sun in the backyard of Jordan's childhood home, a white-painted clapboard house built in the 1940s and distinguished by the graceful porch that stretched the width of the front facing the street. One of the tasks she'd taken over as the weeks dragged on was maintaining her mother's extensive garden that wrapped from the sidewalk out front to the back of the property, gorgeous enough to have starred on several garden tours. It frustrated Mom to be able to do no more than watch her and occasionally try to give her a tutorial in such topics as dividing perennials and mixing the proper strength of fertilizer for hanging baskets, but she'd come so far in only a few months, Jordan had begun to regain an almost lost belief that her mother *would* rebound from the stroke.

After all, she was home, no longer confined to the rehab center, although therapists of various kinds and home health care workers still came daily. So far, Jordan wasn't thinking about looking for work; housecleaning and yard work, plus helping her mother as needed evenings and during the night, was all she could handle. When she said she was happy to be home and to be able to help, she was being completely honest.

She had *not* told her mother about the attack on Elliott or the phone calls from one of the Walla Walla PD detectives.

In fact, her phone vibrated right now and when she glanced down at it, she immediately recognized the number.

"You okay if I leave you for a minute to take this call?" she asked.

"Yah." Her mother's eyes held a speculative expression that she couldn't convey in any other way.

Jordan would rather Mom be suspicious that her daughter had left behind a boyfriend than realize the truth: that she couldn't shake two police detectives who really wanted her to be a viable suspect in an attempted murder.

She let the screen door slam behind her and went deeper into the house to be out of earshot before she answered. "This is Jordan."

The woman's voice told her the caller was Detective Dutton even before she identified herself and then asked, "How's your mom?"

Both detectives had softened up some, Jordan reflected.

"She's doing really well, considering. She needs help to walk and is just learning to shape intelligible words, but considering the severity of her stroke, it's amazing that she's sitting out in her garden right now and we were having a conversation."

"It sounds like this isn't a good time," the detective said stiffly.

"No, it's okay. She can enjoy the sun without struggling so hard to make herself understood. I think it must be frustrating beyond belief." Of all people to confide in.

But she wasn't as surprised as she should have been when Dutton agreed. "My grandmother had a stroke. She… didn't recover, but I remember worrying about whether her brain was working as well as ever while she'd lost the ability to express herself. What if you had an awful itch, or hated the food they were shoveling in your mouth? And I shouldn't have said that."

"No, I've been thinking the same. Fortunately, Mom *is* starting to be able to communicate some of her needs and thoughts. And no, you don't have to tell me that she's at high risk of having a follow-up stroke."

"I've seen people completely recover," the detective said.

If that was a lie, Jordan appreciated it. "This isn't why you called."

"That's…not entirely true. We're not heartless, you know."

Jordan stared blindly at the drawn drapes on her mother's front window. "I do know. I might not be taking your calls if I thought you were."

"Have you heard from Mr. Keefe?"

Her mouth twisted. "No." His silence said it all.

If only he'd heard or seen anything! Police were unsure whether he really hadn't, or whether he could have suffered from some traumatic memory loss. Supposedly, all he did remember was walking into the kitchen from the attached garage and dropping his keys on the counter just before the *bang* of what must have been the gunshot that sent him crashing to the floor. Something slamming into his head was his only other memory until he awakened in the hospital.

If he remembered going into the kitchen, that meant he hadn't forgotten the Fourth of July celebration, or her.

"You're an unlikely suspect," the detective surprised her by saying. "We'd have moved on if it weren't for your, er, history."

"I understand." A familiar, bitter taste filled her mouth. "It will haunt me forever. There's a reason I moved away from Storm Lake, you know. I could see people speculating, even old friends. If people locally hear about what happened to Elliott, wondering will become certainty. My husband—" Oh, how she hated saying that much. His name would be even worse. "He had a bigger personality than I did. He was a star on the football team, had half the girls in high school trailing him through the halls, was comical enough he could get even the teachers to laugh and let him off the hook when he was caught breaking rules."

Soon after their marriage, she'd started noticing his humor had a nasty edge. Or maybe it had changed when he'd begun to resent his first boss, then the one after that, until it became a pattern. He thought *he* should be the supervisor, even though she suspected he slacked off like he had in classes. She didn't dare to so much as hint that anything could be his fault.

She'd be embarrassed that she hadn't seen through him in the first months of her marriage, but she had. It was more that she'd convinced herself things would change, that she had to show her faith in him by sticking through the hard times. She understood that this life wasn't what he'd been so sure he would have. Even after he hit her a few times, then exploded once and came so close to killing her, she desperately convinced herself a family was supposed to stay complete.

Now she suspected that mostly she didn't want anyone to know her judgment had been so bad. She'd almost died because she had been too embarrassed to ignore her pride and say, *You were right, Mom. Help.*

Her mother had been appalled when Jordan announced after high school graduation that instead of going to college, she was marrying Steve Dunn. Once she discovered what a horrible mistake she'd made, Jordan had pretended everything was fine. Eventually, after the traumatic end to her not-quite-twenty-month marriage, she'd figured out that she'd gotten herself in that spot and stayed in it for a lot of complicated reasons she hadn't seen clearly at the time. What she hadn't guessed was how much her pretense would hurt her mother once the truth came out. The result was that Mom blamed herself for Jordan's mistakes.

I was so young, she thought sadly.

"There was nothing out of the ordinary in the weeks before Mr. Keefe was attacked," the detective said. Or was that a question?

"Shouldn't it have been him who noticed anything weird?" Jordan asked.

"He claims the only thing new was that he'd started to date you."

Thank you, Elliott. "He'd gotten a couple of listings that were an especially big deal for him," Jordan said. "He was excited, because he thought he'd taken a step toward being a top seller. He was seeing dollar signs. Somebody could have resented his success."

"We've considered the possibility," the detective said neutrally, "but haven't come up with any, say, sour grapes."

She was talking to Jordan, which was new. Jordan still

didn't believe anything that had happened to her could have led to Elliott being nearly killed, but after a hesitation, she said, "There were a couple of things. Nothing I could prove, and…it just doesn't make sense!"

"A couple of things?"

"I kept feeling like someone was watching me. You know? Just a prickling at the nape of your neck, but when you turn around, no one is there. And then a few days before the Fourth, I thought someone had gotten into my apartment."

"It was unlocked, or a window left open?"

"No. Or, at least, I'm pretty sure I unlocked the front door when I got home from work, but I can't swear to it. You know what it's like when you're juggling stuff you're carrying, including groceries, and you think you turned your key in the lock. The only sign someone had been there was that my butcher knife lay out on the counter." The memory still gave her the creeps. "I'd left the kitchen clean that morning. I swear I did. And I hadn't done any serious cooking, certainly not cutting up meat, for, oh, at least the previous week if not longer. But if I'd called 911, I knew a patrol officer would have stared at the knife and then said, 'Is that yours, ma'am?' I'd admit it was, and he or she would say, 'You don't think you could have been reaching in the drawer where you kept it for something else and maybe just set it aside without thinking?' Could I one hundred percent claim I hadn't? No, but the knives were in one of those wood blocks with slits in them to one side of a deep drawer where I kept linens. I wouldn't have *had* to take one out to reach anything else!"

She still thought it had been a threat, but everything she'd just said would sound so logical to Detective Dutton, Jordan didn't even bother to say that.

"That's it?"

"Somebody bumped me really hard when we were leaving the field after the fireworks display, and I thought whoever it was whispered something in my ear, but I couldn't make it out. And…there was a lot of jostling. You know what a crowd like that is like, even if everyone has had a good time."

There. She'd told them. It probably didn't look good that she hadn't earlier, except they'd have thought then that she had a wild imagination—or that she was trying to divert attention from herself. *Somebody was following her;* he *must have attacked Elliott.*

Sure.

"Well," the detective said with more tact than Jordan might have expected, "we can't check any of that out now. And it is a little hard to see why someone interested in you would go after a man you've gone out with twice. Now, if you had a possessive ex-husband or—boyfriend?"

"My ex-husband was very possessive," Jordan said flatly, "but he's dead. And no, there hasn't been anyone since who gave even an indication of that kind of behavior. Like I told you, I've hardly dated."

There'd been the other stuff over the years: the wedding—and funeral—anniversary cards, and, even worse a couple of times, bouquets that always looked as if they should be set beside a casket at a funeral, or perhaps left on a grave as an annual remembrance. Those would have been expensive, which didn't fit with any of Steve's friends. The handwriting on the cards wasn't always the same, either. The problem was, she could think of several people offhand who had outright accused her of murdering Steve, and then there were the uneasy or even narrow-eyed looks. Steve's brother and mother surely hated her. Maybe his sister; Jordan didn't know. He'd had a big circle of friends, the ones he continued to meet at the tavern evenings after their marriage, when he left her home. People probably thought they were being clever, tormenting her for taking away a man who had been bigger than life, much too good to be the abuser they refused to believe he'd been.

Jordan had given up even bothering to wonder who sent any particular card. She had tried to find out from florists who had ordered the bouquets, but the businesses were determined to honor their customers' privacy, so she gave up asking.

She trashed the flowers and cards alike, refusing to acknowledge how much it hurt to know that so many people in her hometown would rather detest her than believe what was in the police report. Steve had been Somebody, with a capital *S*. Her shyness and the self-doubt that took deep root the day her father had left and never bothered with her again had combined to turn her into a nonentity in most people's eyes. She even understood that; it had taken her years to discover who she really was.

Detective Dutton didn't comment on Jordan's teenage marriage that had ended so catastrophically after twenty months. She'd likely seen enough on her job to be able to read between the lines on that report. Unfortunately, she and her partner could have convinced themselves that, after being battered, Jordan might have nursed underlying rage and developed a taste for offing men who'd maybe said or done the wrong thing.

That was her, she thought: the angel of death.

The detective didn't try to extend today's conversation.

Jordan forgot all about it after she hurried out the back door to find her mother tipped so far in the chair, she was inches from tumbling to the brick pavers.

After gently helping Mom into the closest to a sitting

position she could achieve, Jordan caught her breath and vowed not to take her eyes off her mother for more than a minute unless she was safely tucked into bed with a bolster of pillows that kept her from rolling off the mattress.

So much for confiding in a supposedly sympathetic police detective.

AS WAS PROBABLY INEVITABLE, Shelly Hendrick's recovery slowed. Jordan was aware of very little that lay outside her childhood home, her mother's garden, the physical therapists, the city swimming pool where she took part in a water aerobics class aimed to help physically challenged people. The pharmacy—Jordan was on good terms with both the pharmacist and an assistant she'd known in school who seemed happy to see her and genuinely regretful about her mother's stroke. The grocery store, the several home care workers who came and went. Oh, and the couple of different doctors Mom saw on a regular basis.

The local hospital served as a regional center for specialists. Her mother had been lucky in that respect. A neurologist had taken over from the trauma team quickly. Mom's family doctor stayed in the loop, along with a cardiologist, a rehab nurse, physical and occupational therapist, a speech pathologist and a case manager. Jordan had been assured that a psychologist or even psychiatrist might be a big help once her mother's speech improved enough.

Jordan was grateful for every one of them, although she couldn't help being appalled by the bills. The many tests, from an MRI to a cerebral angiogram, did not come cheap. So far, Mom's insurance was paying the bulk of the bills, but taking care of what was left could still end up totally depleting her funds.

Her mother was currently undergoing an echocardiogram

for the second time, as the doctors had never been entirely satisfied that they had identified the source of the clot or clots that had traveled to the brain and caused the stroke. Jordan sat in the waiting room, scrolling through news on her phone without getting very engaged when she heard a voice.

"Jordan Hendrick!"

She looked up and recognized one of the ER doctors who'd checked in several times while Mom was still hospitalized to see how she was doing. She'd wondered at the time whether big-city docs ever did anything like that.

Now she smiled. "Dr. Parnell. How nice to see you. Mom's having another echocardiogram, thus me sitting here twiddling my thumbs."

"Make it Colin," he said, lowering himself to the seat right beside her. "I'm not your mother's doctor anymore."

She blinked. Was that a glint of interest in his brown eyes?

"Colin," she agreed. "Did you just happen to wander this way?"

He laughed, making her realize that he was an attractive man. When she'd briefly met him before, all she'd seen was the white coat and stethoscope. The physicians all blended together at that point.

"No, I heard your mother would be here and thought I'd say hello to you. Find out how you're holding up."

"I'm not the one struggling. That's Mom. People keep telling me she's progressing well, but…oh, she is. It's just so slow."

He laid a warm hand atop hers on the armrest of the chair. "I know. But it hasn't even been three months, and she's home. From what I've been told, she really is bouncing back faster than we originally expected. She was young to have a massive stroke."

"I know, especially when she didn't have any obvious risk factors."

His eyebrows rose. "She'd been ignoring her higher-than-ideal blood pressure and what we now know was atrial fibrillation."

Jordan made a face. "She was sure her symptoms had to do with the amount of coffee she drank."

"She's not the first person and won't be the last I've heard that from."

His hand remained atop hers. She didn't quite know how to react.

"I'd suggest we go get a cup of coffee, but I don't suppose you have time," he said.

Was that a tiny thrill of anticipation, or dread? "I'm afraid not," Jordan said. "She should be out pretty soon."

"Are you able to get away long enough to meet for coffee another time, or even to go out for dinner?" he asked.

"I…maybe?"

He laughed. "A solid answer."

How could she not laugh, too? Impulse seized her. "Sure. Why don't we start with coffee so I don't have to leave my mother for too long?" Good excuse.

"Tomorrow?" he said immediately, taking out his phone and pulling up the calendar. "Say, three o'clock?"

She did the same. "I can do that. Mom's physical therapist will be there, and then an aide takes over to help her shower."

"Great." He was especially handsome when he grinned at her and squeezed her hand before rising to his feet. "Clearwater Café?"

A trendy—by Storm Lake standards—establishment, the café was only a few blocks from the hospital and had both good food and coffee, so she said, "That sounds great. Thanks for suggesting it."

His name was called over the PA system just then. He shook his head in mock dismay and left at a brisk pace.

Not until he was gone did she wonder whether this was smart, given her recent history. She wondered whether anybody had told him she was at the heart of one of Storm Lake's most shocking tragedies, one that nobody seemed to have forgotten.

I should cancel, she thought—but the two of them weren't planning to go out on the town. It would be the merest chance if anyone who held a grudge against her happened to see her sipping coffee and chatting with a doctor she obviously knew from the hospital. And what was she supposed to do? Quit trying to have a semi-normal life because of the assault on Elliott Keefer? The one Jordan couldn't believe was connected to her?

No, that was ridiculous. She'd been home for months. Wasn't she entitled to start *some* kind of social life?

Still, she circled back to thinking maybe going out with anyone right now wasn't a good idea, then feeling mad because there wasn't any good reason she shouldn't…until a nurse pushing her mother in a wheelchair came through the double doors.

"She's all set to go home!" the nurse declared. "Dr. Taylor says she'll give you a call to talk about what she saw. Why don't you go get your car, and we'll meet you at the portico?"

"I'll do that." Jordan bent to kiss her mother's cheek, then hurried toward the main entrance so Mom wouldn't have to wait long.

Chapter Four

It was one date. No need to panic.

Still, Jordan sat stiffly in the passenger seat beside Dr. Colin Parnell and thought, *I shouldn't be doing this*.

She also wished she could drop the "doctor" part in her mind. She would *not* let herself feel the inadequacy that had haunted her as a teenager. She was working toward a BA. It was just taking time.

What if he didn't see her as an equal and was thinking about nothing but getting her into bed?

He'd be in for a big disappointment. She'd worked hard on herself to accept that, while she'd made one massively bad choice, she'd also proved her strength by surviving. Heck, she bet her personal life had been more colorful than Colin Parnell's.

"What are you thinking?" he asked just then.

"I'm giving myself a pep talk," she admitted. "This will be the longest I've left Mom since she had the stroke." Nice excuse.

"You said you found an aide to stay with her."

"Yes, and Mom's doing really well. She kept telling me she didn't need anyone, but even with the cane she walks so unsteadily I keep being afraid she'll fall." Jordan sighed. "Enough about Mom, already."

He laughed. "I can agree with that, although if you need to talk about her, I'm available."

"Nope. I'm ready to expand my horizons." Just…not too far.

He'd asked her if she liked Italian food, and minutes later they walked into a small restaurant in a space that had been a dry-cleaning business in her day. The smell was amazing, and her first quick scan of diners didn't identify anyone she knew. She let herself relax.

After shedding their coats, they were seated at a table in the corner. The fat candle added to a romantic ambiance created in part by dim lighting. After they ordered and their waiter poured a red wine Colin had chosen, he lifted his glass and said, "To getting to know you."

She lifted hers as well and smiled. "To getting to know *you*."

They'd covered some ground over coffee last week. Jordan knew he had grown up in Idaho Falls and had always intended to come back to the area to practice medicine. What she didn't know was whether anybody had whispered to him about the scandal that had shaped her life.

"Do you plan to stay in town once your mother is more solidly on her feet?" he asked now, dipping a slice of bread in the spiced olive oil. His mouth quirked.

She frowned a little at his question. "I actually haven't even thought about future plans. I was so focused on being here for Mom, and then the slow pace of her recovery makes it obvious that at best I can't leave her anytime in the foreseeable future. So…I don't know." Her frown deepened. Strange she hadn't let herself think about this. Being home in Storm Lake stirred up a lot of complicated stuff, much of it bad, but she was rediscovering how much she loved, too, starting with the wooded, mountainous setting on a beautiful lake. It really did feel like home. "Some of the issues I didn't like here have probably changed," she said slowly. "Right now, I can't see myself moving out of the area and leaving Mom behind. I mean, realistically…"

He obviously knew what she was thinking.

She got him talking about why he'd chosen trauma as a medical specialty and found he could be really funny when confessing to his youthful exploration of adrenaline-inducing activities, from jumping onto a backyard trampoline from a second-story window in his parents' house to amateur bungee jumping.

She was laughing when the restaurant door opened and a couple entered. She froze mid-breath. Guy Feller, with a woman who was probably his wife.

Maybe because she was staring, he saw her right away and met her eyes.

Surely he'd be civil, if he spoke to her at all. Crossing her fingers out of sight, she wanted to believe that.

In fact, once he and the woman had been shown to a table, he murmured something to her and steered her toward Jordan.

Tall and lean, he'd matured well, she thought. She could see the boy she'd known best only because they'd gone all the way through school together.

"Guy," she said pleasantly. "How nice to see you. Your mother talks about you."

Colin stood and the two men shook hands, introducing themselves as well as Guy's wife, Autumn.

"I know I've told you about Jordan," he said to her as she smiled politely.

Determined to keep it light, Jordan asked, "Did you tell her about the birthday party when I turned—what was it?

Eight? Nine?—and you stayed with your back to a wall staring at your feet for something like two hours?"

His laugh appeared genuine. "Yeah, I was paralyzed. All those *girls*."

Jordan grinned.

"In fairness, I did bring a present—"

"Which your mother undoubtedly chose and wrapped."

"And I ate cake and ice cream."

"Hunched over it while you pretended no one else was there."

"C'mon." He appealed to Colin. "How would you have felt about being the only boy at a birthday party with a gaggle of girls all dressed in pink and giggling nonstop?"

"I'd have been out of there," admitted the man who'd just told her how much he enjoyed risking his life.

Jordan rolled her eyes.

"Pleasure to meet you," Guy told Colin, then looked steadily at Jordan. "I wasn't as good a friend to you as I should have been. I…regret that."

Stunned, she bobbed her head.

He didn't give his wife or Colin a chance to ask what he meant, and even though she saw questions in Colin's eyes, he didn't pry.

Instead, they returned to the "getting to know each other" conversation that Jordan tried hard to keep superficial.

Still, she was surprised to realize what a good time she was having with the doctor and didn't feel too nervous about him delivering her to her doorstep. Dr. Colin Parnell wasn't a man to be pushy, she felt sure. To the contrary, she suspected he wielded patience, that charming smile and his innate kindness to achieve his aim when it came to women.

He did kiss her on her front porch, but gently. "I have this feeling you've been burned," he said quietly, confirming her belief when he raised his head. "I had a good time tonight."

"I did, too," she was able to say honestly.

He pressed his lips to her forehead, said, "I'll call," and strolled back to his car.

She waved before she let herself into the house. The evening had left her with way too much to think about—but that would have to wait until she'd seen the aide out and reported to Mom.

JORDAN SLEPT BETTER than she had in a while. Getting out, laughing, forgetting for a couple of hours the main preoccupation of her life, was better than a sleeping pill. Mom must have made it through the night, too.

Wait. What if she'd decided to get up to go to the bathroom on her own? She was definitely starting to rebel against the "don't move without someone standing beside you" rule. In one way, that was good news, but in another…

Jordan leaped up, feeling some relief because she didn't find Mom lying in the hall or the bathroom. Mom's bedroom door was always partially open, and…there she was, awake and reaching for the bell that sat on her bedside stand.

Jordan stepped into the room. "Good morning! Do you need a hand?"

"No." Her ever-stubborn mother slowly pushed herself into a sitting position, albeit twisted to accommodate her weak side, then swung her feet onto the floor. Her walker waited to give her support standing. Once she was upright, she said, "Hah! Told you."

"Yeah, you did." Jordan grabbed her robe and draped it over the walker as Mom shuffled toward the bathroom. Thank goodness this was mostly a one-story house, the attic reserved for storage. Stairs would have been impossible for Mom to navigate now.

Ear cocked for any worrisome thuds or crashes behind her, Jordan went on to the kitchen, letting her mother follow. Loss of independence was a big trigger for depression in stroke victims. She didn't want to contribute.

They both had coffee. Jordan sliced the banana that went on top of each of their bowls of cereal, since her mother's right hand was still both weak and frozen into an unfortunately clawlike position. It had improved noticeably, though, after a whole lot of PT. Life would be easier for Mom if the stroke had crippled her left side instead of her more dominant right.

"How…was…your date?"

"Good," she said. "Do you remember Dr. Parnell?"

"Yah." Mom's tongue still refused to form the *S* sound. Mostly, Jordan's brain simply filled it in. "Nice."

She chatted about dinner, how good the food was— Mom had lunch with friends regularly but had never been to the restaurant—and mentioned seeing Guy Feller. The two of them laughed again at the memory of the birthday party that had severed the friendship. Jordan still remembered the doll his mother had picked out to give her, and the beet-red color that crept over Guy's cheeks while she was opening it.

An hour later, the doorbell rang and Jordan let in the aide who helped Mom take a shower. Later today, Mom's hairdresser was going to drop by, too, which she was excited about.

Jordan took advantage of the time to work outside, starting by raking leaves. After checking to find an occupational therapist with Mom, she continued her ongoing task of cutting back brown stems of perennials and annuals and then

mulching flower beds—sort of like piling on the comfort-
ers—in preparation for the really cold weather to come.
Late October teetered between the heat of summer and the
bitter cold of winter in mountainous Idaho. The electric
bill was climbing by the day, she reflected, but at least the
water bill had plummeted now that she was no longer laying out soaker hoses for the forty-something roses in Mom's
garden. In fact, the hoses were now curled up neatly in the
garage; if left out, they'd crack over the winter.

Jordan had grown up rolling her eyes at Mom's over-the-
top enthusiasm for gardening. Since she'd gotten home, she'd
taken on the work so that when Mom made it home from
the hospital, her garden would be brilliant with bloom and
welcoming. Now…maybe it was odd, but Jordan had become invested.

Lunch was sandwiches, applesauce and chips—so
imaginative—and Jordan had put the pillow bolster into
place once her mother had lain down for a nap when the
doorbell rang again.

Who on earth? Jordan had bought a whiteboard calendar to keep track of her mother's many appointments. Had
she forgotten to note one?

She didn't even think of looking to see who was here
before she opened the door. All-too-familiar shock struck
her at the sight of two uniformed police officers on the
doorstep. And, dear God, wasn't one of them Cody Bussert, better known in high school as Buzz? Jordan had had
no idea that one of Steve's good buddies had become a cop.

Apprehension had her clutching the door. "I…how can
I help you? My mother is—"

Cody interrupted without apparent compunction. "It's
you we need to talk to, *Ms*. Hendrick."

The other officer glanced at his partner in what appeared

to be surprise and possibly warning. Had to be the sneer in *Buzz's* voice.

It made her mad enough that she was able to say coolly, "And why would that be?"

The second cop said, "I'm Officer Wilson. This is—"

"She knows me," Buzz snapped.

"May we come in?"

Jordan glanced over her shoulder. "Can we talk on the porch? My mother had a stroke recently and is napping."

"I'm sorry," Officer Wilson said. "That's tough. Yes, we can sit out here."

Thank goodness the day was cool but not bitingly cold so she didn't have to ask them in. Buzz leaned a hip against the porch railing while his partner perched on an Adirondack chair, obviously not wanting to slide far enough back as to impede his being able to leap up to…? Tackle her? Pull his weapon?

Pulse racing, she sat on the swing hanging from chains. "What is it? I haven't been back in town long—"

"And another man is already dead," Buzz said with a razor-sharp edge in his voice.

Her fingernails bit into her palms. "What?"

Officer Wilson looked reprovingly at Bussert, but said, "We're speaking with people who knew Dr. Colin Parnell well."

Knew. Past tense. It couldn't be.

"You mean, he's… Something happened to him?" That sounded mealy-mouthed, but she couldn't even let herself picture—

"I'm afraid he was murdered last night, Ms. Hendrick."

"Oh my God." This couldn't be. She heard herself whimpering, "Oh…my God."

"I believe you and he went out together yesterday evening."

Panic clogged her throat. She couldn't let them see anything but the grief, not now, not until she had time to think about what this meant. "Yes. We…had dinner. He dropped me here afterward."

Why hadn't she said no? Why, *why*?

"Do you know what time?"

"About eight thirty." The pressure behind her sternum *hurt*. "I'd hired an aide to stay with Mom and promised not to be out late."

"Someone was here when you arrived."

"Yes. She…was in the living room. She saw Colin and smiled and waved. He wished her good-night, too. I guess their paths have crossed before."

A small spiral notebook had materialized in Officer Wilson's hand. *Small town, low tech.* "Her name?" he asked.

"Uh… Patty Younger. She's one of Mom's and my favorites."

The questions went on and on. How had she met Colin? Hospital. How long ago? Three months. Had they been dating that entire time? No. She explained about the most recent encounter with him at the hospital while she waited for her mother who was undergoing a test, about the casual invitation to coffee, then dinner. Yes, she'd seen someone she knew at the restaurant. Buzz obviously recognized Guy's name.

Colin had kissed her lightly on her doorstep. Yes, that was the first time. No, except for the two occasions, she'd never seen him outside the hospital. She had no idea where he lived.

They didn't tell her. But how hard was it these days to find someone's address online?

Only at the end did they allow her to ask, "Was he killed at home? Or…or did he stop somewhere else?" Had a bullet from a high-powered rifle struck him as he was driving? As horrible as all this was, she prayed his death didn't resemble the attacks on Pete and Elliott. Because if it did…

She would have to tell these cops before they found out on their own.

"He was attacked in his own home," Officer Wilson said stiffly.

"You mean…someone was waiting for him?"

"It appears he'd been home long enough to make a cup of coffee and settle down in a home office to work on his laptop."

Had his assailant already been in the house? Hidden, so as to muddy Jordan's alibi? Oh, that made sense.

She could see the attack with painful clarity. Had he been shot first, or had a blow to his head that came from behind taken him down? Weirdly, that was the moment when grief struck like a lightning bolt. She saw him, kind eyes, handsome face, the dimple that formed in one cheek when he laughed, which she thought he did often. His stories, a quality she could only think of as joy in life.

Had he really been killed because of *her*? How was she supposed to live with that?

"The caliber of bullet that killed Dr. Parnell was the same as the bullet that killed your husband," Buzz said, and the expression in his eyes spoke for him. "What happened to that gun after his death?"

Even though she was afraid hot tears were dripping down her cheeks, Jordan held her head high and spoke with as much steel in her voice as she could summon. "I have no idea. I never wanted to see it again. That's something you should be able to look up. What's more, as a police officer, you have access to reports about Steve's death. Not a single person, from responding officers to the doctors, believed I shot him for any reason but self-defense. He had been abusive in different ways almost from the beginning of our marriage. And yes, I should have left him before it came to that, but you have no right to hear the reasons I didn't. The man you knew was not the man I had to live with."

His glare didn't soften.

She transferred her gaze to the other officer. "Was Dr. Parnell…beaten, too?"

Wilson's expression sharpened. "Yes."

If they threw her in jail, what would Mom do? But she had to tell them. They'd inevitably find out anyway.

"I told you I don't know where Colin lives." *Lived.* "Except to save my life, I have never committed a violent act in my life. But…" She took a deep breath. "I think his murder may have to do with me."

Chapter Five

The interrogation that followed was a nightmare. It made her realize how incredibly lucky she'd been with the detectives in Walla Walla. They, at least, started as impartial. Once Detectives Shannon and Dutton heard from the Storm Lake PD, though, their opinions about her would probably do a one-eighty.

Thinking of them, Jordan asked, "Shouldn't I be talking to a detective?"

The two men exchanged a glance. Wilson answered, "In a small department like this, we all step into major investigations. I'm…expecting a promotion to detective anytime, so I'm sure the chief will leave me on this anyway."

It wasn't him she wanted to get rid of. It was Buzz, who made no pretense of hiding his opinion of her.

She had her chance when he asked an especially offensive question. Rising to her feet and completely ignoring him, she looked at Wilson.

"As you may have gathered, your partner holds a grudge against me because he was friends in high school with my husband. Apparently—" now she allowed herself a scathing glance at the jerk "—he still believes because Steve was a football star, the life of the party and a popular man on campus, he couldn't have had a darker side. I will not speak with Officer Bussert again."

Buzz said nastily, "What makes you think you have any choice?"

She raised a hand, her gaze once again on Officer Wilson, who stood, too. "I won't talk to anyone again without having a lawyer present. I did not commit these crimes. As I told you, I believe I've been stalked on and off all these years by someone who blames me for my husband's death. Someone—" she made this stare incinerating "—who has a lot in common with Officer Bussert."

Officer Wilson winced.

"Yet you kept no evidence of that stalking," Buzz sneered.

"Now, you'll have to excuse me—"

"Wait! You said you'd give me the names of the investigators in Walla Walla and their phone numbers. I'm sure I could track them down, but…"

"Give me a minute." She hustled into the house, careful not to let the screen door slam, grabbed her phone, and pulled up the names and numbers by the time she was back out on the porch.

Wilson scrawled the info on his pad. "Thank you. I'll be in touch."

At least he'd said *I* rather than *we*. She kept her mouth shut, just watched as they retreated to their patrol unit and drove away. Then she waved a weak hand at a neighbor who was out raking—but mostly watching the excitement—and retreated back into the house.

No, a sob was building in her chest. She'd wake her mother. She hurried out the back door, a hand clapped over her face. Only after she dropped into a bench as far from the house as possible did she let the wail erupt.

"I'M NOT REAL happy about this," said the Storm Lake police chief, Tom's new boss. His call had come in while Tom was packing his last possessions to vacate his condo, which he'd let out for the next year. "Even though we're past the tourist season, we need you fully on board, but this case is a strange one."

Hip and thigh aching, Tom pulled up a barstool that he was leaving for the young couple moving in. "Tell me about it," he said.

Chief Guthrie had decided it was ideal that Tom would be moving into town now, knowing no one. "Place this size, we couldn't usually pull off any kind of undercover operation. But the house almost across the street from the suspect is up for rent. Decent place, too—you might want to stay in it."

Tom had done a couple of undercover stints in his career and hated both of them, so his first feeling wasn't positive. That said, this might give him a little longer before he had to participate in any hard physical operation—say, a search and rescue.

So he made an inquiring noise.

The facts Guthrie presented about a woman who seemed to leave dead men behind everywhere she went created a strange picture in Tom's mind. The chief wasn't kidding. Jordan Hendrick, age twenty-eight, had married right out of high school. The husband had allegedly been abusive. She'd shot and killed him to save her own life. In fact, she'd spent days in the hospital recovering from the damage he'd done to her in that struggle.

"At the time, I believed her story," Guthrie admitted, before continuing.

She moved away, first to Great Falls, Montana, then to Walla Walla, a smallish city in eastern Washington, staying off the radar until roughly three years ago. At that point, a man she'd just started dating was killed in an apparent home invasion. Five months ago, she started seeing another lucky guy, who after the second date was attacked and nearly killed in his own home. The investigators there couldn't pin anything on her but were uneasy. Her mother had a stroke, and this Hendrick woman rushed home to take care of her. Unlikely she'd had time for any social life at first, the chief said, but just recently, she'd gone out with a doctor from the hospital. A week later, they had dinner—and he was attacked and killed in his own home later that same evening.

"We have no witnesses, no trace evidence leading to her, but I'm not a real big fan of coincidence," Chief Guthrie said. "We don't have a ballistics report back yet, so we don't know if the same gun was used here and in Walla Walla. The detective I spoke to there said different guns were used in the murder of the one man and the attempted murder of the other."

Coincidence didn't sit well with Tom, either. Still, a woman in her twenties made an unlikely serial killer. Unlike the classic black widow, she apparently hadn't gained a thing from any of these deaths. She claimed a stalker but had zero proof. Somehow, she'd never been disturbed enough by the strange messages left on her doorstep and in her mailbox over the years to bother calling 911 to report any of them.

The two men threw around the possibility she'd left behind other victims who hadn't been linked to her. There were some big gaps in time to be accounted for.

"It was hiring you that gave me the idea," Guthrie said. "You'd be in a good position to watch her. Not saying you should push it too far, but with a little luck, you might make friends with her. I can't think of any other way to be proactive."

What he meant was, at thirty-four, Tom was close enough in age to their target to potentially appeal to her. In the end, Tom agreed. It sounded like a soft assignment, but intriguing. After ending the call, to give himself something to go on, he looked up Jordan Hendrick's Washington State driver's license, since she didn't appear to have gotten one in Idaho yet, but the photo didn't tell him much. Blond hair—although he squinted and wasn't so sure that was quite right, brown eyes, five feet five, 120 pounds. Weight on a driver's license was almost always about as accurate as a carnival psychic's predictions. She was a pretty woman, he thought, but given the quality of DMV photos, he couldn't even be sure about that.

He had a feeling Chief Guthrie was hoping for more than a casual friendship sparking between his new detective and this black widow. If he could persuade her into a date or two, a trap would be a logical tactic.

Then he'd only have to worry about surviving a relationship with Jordan Hendrick.

JORDAN IDLY NOTICED a moving truck in the driveway of a house on the other side of the street that had been vacant and for sale since she'd come home. Men unloaded, but she didn't catch sight of anyone who was an obvious new homeowner. No children were running around, anyway. She didn't see a woman.

She wouldn't have paid any attention at all if not for her mother, who could hardly wait to find out all. Mom knew everyone on the block, and despite Jordan's new notoriety, most of them stopped by to chat when Mom was out front or dropped by with offerings of baked goods on a pretty regular basis. Mrs. Chung, a tiny woman in her eighties who was almost as ardent a gardener as Jordan's mother, had been the first to visit her in the hospital.

They'd all carefully stayed neutral where Jordan was concerned, for which she was grateful. Despite rampant gossip, in the days following the murder, they continued to stop by for her mother's sake. They smiled even at Jordan, commented on the weather or asked in low voices how her mother was really doing before spending time with Mom. But Jordan knew *they* knew she was being investigated by the police, and neither they nor she could ever forget that.

The facade of normalcy was almost unbearable.

The Storm Lake police had made it clear they expected her to stay put and available. Not like she'd flee anyway; she couldn't leave her mother. What she knew was that her life had taken another hard left turn. Steve's death, she'd come to terms with. But what happened to Pete Schroder, Elliott, Colin was a horror that weighed on her every waking minute.

Whenever she had an idle moment, she tried to remember everyone who might possibly be responsible for trying to set her up as a murderess, but how could she separate the burning stares that might have held hate from the snubs that might have grown into more if she'd stayed around? Then there were the doubtful glances, the avid ones, the… She shuddered every time she circled through her memories of those expressions, those faces.

She would never dare again have even a friendship with a man. Unless and until the police identified and arrested the killer—and how likely was that when they focused on her?—the future she'd still sometimes imagined, in which she had a husband and children, had faded from sight like an oasis in the desert that never had been real.

Desperate for occupation, she began to wish there was more to do in the garden, but she'd already divided perennials. With it now November, in the next few weeks she could plant more bulbs, but that was about it. The next big job wasn't until March when she'd be pruning roses for the first time in her life. If she wasn't in jail by then.

She'd started running again but could only do that when someone was here with Mom. Today was relatively balmy for the season, so she'd put on a parka but didn't bother to zip it, and sat on the porch with a book on her lap. With fragmented concentration, she was easily distracted by the sight of a man emerging from the house recently visited by the moving truck. He gave her something new to think about.

He walked down the driveway, his head turned as he seemed to ponder where he wanted to go, and then he ambled along the sidewalk toward his next-door neighbor, going up to knock on the door. He disappeared inside for long enough to suggest he'd sat down for a cup of coffee. When he reappeared, he progressed to the next house on his side of the street.

Jordan rolled her eyes at her nosiness, but what else did she have to do? Once Mom was up from her nap, she'd want every detail Jordan could glean about this new neighbor.

On a block occupied mostly by senior citizens who'd been in these houses as long as her mother had, this guy stood out by his youth alone. Youth being relative. Jordan guessed him to be in his early to midthirties. He was also tall, broad-shouldered and...not quite handsome, at least from this distance, but something. Quintessentially male, she decided—and, after all, she had plenty of time on her hands to watch him. She'd have guessed him to be athletic except that his walk was noticeably stiff even though he didn't let whatever bothered him shorten his long strides.

After sitting on the porch with Mrs. Chung for an interval, he apparently caught sight of Jordan, because he strode across the street directly toward her, his gaze intent on her.

She didn't move, just waited until he reached the foot of the porch steps. Short, unruly brown hair and piercing blue eyes added to her impression of a man who didn't have to be model-handsome to catch any woman's eyes.

She wouldn't let *any* man catch her eye.

"Hi," he said. "I just moved in across the street."

There was no reason not to be polite. "The moving truck made you the talk of the neighborhood. People were starting to wonder if the house would ever sell."

"It didn't. I guess the owners gave up. I'm renting, although if I like my new job and the town, I have the option to buy." He paused, looking up at her. "I'm Tom Moore."

"Jordan Hendrick. This is actually my mother's house. You may not see much of her, because she's recovering from a stroke and still doesn't get around very well. I'm in town to take care of her."

He smiled, planted a foot on the bottom step and leaned a hip against the railing. "She's lucky you could drop everything and come home."

He had a deep, resonant voice that Jordan did not want to find appealing.

"Mom's always been there for me," she said simply.

He nodded as if he understood.

The pause became a little awkward. Obviously, he was in no hurry to move on. It appeared he didn't yet know he was speaking to a murder suspect. She'd have to thank Mrs. Chung and Mr. Griffin later for not giving him a heads-up.

"What's your new job?" she asked.

"I'm with the county parks. I moved here from San Francisco, a city I enjoyed, and which has fantastic parks, but like your mother I'm recuperating, although in my case from an injury. The hills in San Francisco, not to mention the beaches, challenged my physical capability. I thought this would be a change of pace, and I could look forward to some hiking and climbing down the line. Maybe take up cross-country skiing."

She didn't feel like she should ask *how* he'd gotten hurt. He could volunteer that if he wanted her to know.

When she didn't comment, he finally withdrew his booted foot from the step.

"I'll let you get back to your book. Just wanted to introduce myself. If I can give you a hand anytime, I'm close by."

"Thank you, but we have a constant stream of health aides and therapists of one kind or another coming and going."

"You an only child?"

Her mouth tightened, but she saw no reason not to say, "Yes."

She was being rude not to take him up on his conversational gambits, she knew she was, but Jordan wasn't trying to make new friends, and particularly with a man. *Any* man.

A flicker in his eyes told her he knew she was just waiting for him to go away, and he bent his head. "I may see you around."

"I'm sure you will," she said, sounding stilted.

He studied her for another few seconds, smiled faintly and turned to walk away.

Message sent and received.

WELL, HIS FRIENDLY introduction had pancaked. Ms. Hendrick was not receptive to a new neighbor who wanted to become buddies. Tom would like to think she'd been as aware of him as a man as he'd been of her as a woman, but he was honest enough with himself to admit he had no idea. The whole conversation had been forced.

She was probably wondering why a guy his age was trying to get chummy with all his neighbors. Which was actually a good question. He'd never done more than nod with most of his neighbors in the tall brick warehouse in San Francisco that had been converted to condominiums. A guy his age met people at work, bars or the health club.

He had to assume she was watching, which meant he went on to talk with an old guy next door who either needed hearing aids desperately or didn't bother wearing them when he didn't expect a caller. After tearing himself away and bellowing, "Nice to meet you!" Tom crossed the street and let himself into his own new home.

He'd brought most of his furniture, but that familiarity didn't make the house feel homey. Furniture wasn't in the right place. Neither were light switches, or the dishwasher, which was strangely placed an irritating distance from the kitchen sink.

He liked the era of the house—1940s, at a guess, along with the others on this block. There was a solidity to it. If he were really to buy it, he'd want to do some serious re-modeling, though, starting with the bathrooms. It might be worth spending the money, at the very least, to get a plumber out here to replace the showerhead so he could have a satisfying shower.

Tom sighed and walked far enough into the living room to allow him to stand mostly hidden by the drapes but be able to look across the street and down one house. He thought his target hadn't moved.

Frowning, he mulled over his impressions of the woman. *Stricken* was the first word that came to mind. As he'd

approached, he had the impression she wasn't really reading. She looked like someone emotionally paralyzed. That
could be true whether she was guilty of these crimes or not.
Being under scrutiny by law enforcement wasn't a lot of
fun. There were plenty of times he'd done his best to lay
on the pressure, waiting for his suspect to crack.

Tom winced. Wasn't that what he and Max had done
with that last investigation? Jared Smith had cracked, all
right, and come out firing.

Tom thought what he'd seen in her eyes was pain, but
he couldn't put any weight behind what might be a trick of
the light. Preliminary impressions were just that.

Fortunately or unfortunately, he wasn't sure which, he
could say with certainty that she was more than pretty. The
delicacy of her features hadn't been shown to best advantage in that DMV photo. Her slender wrists and graceful
neck made him think she was fine-boned overall. He'd been
right about her hair, thick and shiny, sort of a streaky dish-
water blond that she wore bundled in a knot on the back
of her head. Curves, undetermined. Her brown eyes were
more caramel than dark chocolate. He felt sure she hadn't
worn any makeup at all, and in his opinion didn't need it.

He didn't like the complication of having his body stir
just because he was picturing her. On the other hand, he
wasn't good at faking attraction, and he couldn't expect a
reciprocal response without laying it out there.

Frowning at where she sat, still unmoving, he tried to
decide a next step. Asking her out…yeah, no. As a renter,
he was expected to keep up the yard, but it was pretty bare.
Casual encounters would be tough. He had no flower beds,
like the ones that wrapped her house, and several of the
others on the block, too. He definitely needed to rake the
leaves blanketing the lawn out front, which would make

him visible from her house, but he'd save that for tomorrow. Actually, a couple of old fruit trees in the fenced backyard had dropped most of their leaves, too, but he'd be out of sight working there.

He had to keep active, Tom reminded himself. He'd brought weights and a treadmill, and was thinking of buying a rowing machine, too. If there were any indication Ms. Hendrick belonged to a gym, he'd have taken that route, but Chief Guthrie said no. Maybe she'd turn out to be a runner, and he could casually meet up with her.

His main intent was to stay alert so he could be sure she wasn't slipping out once her mother slept come evening. He doubted that would happen, given the police scrutiny, but he bet she hated feeling watched.

His number one priority was making sure she didn't notice that she had a new watcher—right across the street.

And he needed to be patient. There was no big hurry here, not unless she got involved with another man.

Chapter Six

Didn't it figure that Mom decided she had to meet the new neighbor?

"We should do something to welcome him," she declared—or at least that's how Jordan translated her speech. "Bake cookies."

Bake cookies. Okay, she couldn't misunderstand that.

"Mom, I'm sure it's not necessary."

Her mother firmly disagreed. Taking a casserole or cookies to a newcomer was part and parcel of belonging in this neighborhood.

In fairness, Jordan had seen others on the block knocking on Tom Moore's doorstep and handing him something.

All she could do was make a face behind Mom's back before pulling out a cookbook with familiar tattered pages.

Snickerdoodles, she decided, after determining she had all the ingredients.

The baking part actually turned out to be fun. She let her mother do everything she could while seated, even if that took way longer. A double batch meant they could enjoy home-baked goodies. Uh, not that they'd been short of them thanks to Mom's friends and neighbors, but still.

Once the cookies had cooled and Jordan had climbed on a step stool to unearth some round tins with lids to hold them, Mom also announced that she wanted to walk over to deliver the "welcome to the neighborhood" cookies.

"Mom! That's farther than it looks."

Her mother's facial muscles had recovered enough to let her almost raise an eyebrow. And it was true that the therapists were encouraging her to walk. Jordan checked to see that Tom Moore's big black SUV was parked in his driveway. Probably his single garage was too small for a monster vehicle like that.

Today was chilly enough, Jordan bundled her mother up as if she were a toddler, threw on her own parka and led the way. The first obstacle was crossing the threshold with the walker. That the recently built ramp was at the back of the house meant it took them a good ten minutes to reach the front walkway.

Down the driveway, onto the street. The pace slowed. Taking mini-steps, Jordan looked from one direction to the other and hoped no teenager would rocket down their block right now.

"Doing okay, Mom?"

"'Course."

Okey doke.

The new neighbor must have glanced out a window because he appeared on his porch, grabbed a rocking chair and carried it down to the walkway. Evidently sharing her concern, he turned his head sharply at the sound of a car engine not too far away, but no vehicle appeared.

He called, "I hope this means you're coming to see me, Mrs. Hendrick." Smiling eyes met Jordan's. "And you, Jordan."

"We are. Mom, this is Tom Moore, who I told you about." She touched her mother's back. "Let's get out of the road, why don't we."

Mom shuffled forward. Jordan noticed how, without making a big deal out of it, Tom moved in close on her mother's other side, probably as ready to grab her as he was. That was…nice, she couldn't help thinking.

Mom sat with obvious relief and a little help in the chair he'd provided.

"I can get something for us to sit on—" he began, but Jordan shook her head.

"Ground's fine for me." She did hand over the tin of cookies. "Snickerdoodles. I hope you like them." She sat cross-legged on the cold but fortunately dry grass.

"I love them." He sat, too, but stretched out his long legs. He grinned. "Friendly neighborhood. I may have to let out my belt if people keep bringing food."

He asked her mother how long she'd lived here, and at least pretended to understand her answer. Jordan stayed, watchful, to one side. Mom struggled to ask something, and he told her he'd never been to Idaho until a week ago; he'd grown up in northern California—McKinleyville in Humboldt County, which Jordan recalled had once been famous for illegal marijuana farms—then gone to college in San Francisco and worked there ever since.

He opened the tin of cookies and offered them each one. Mom took one with apparent pleasure. She tended to dribble crumbs when she ate, but Tom gave no sign of noticing. Fortunately, Jordan had a tissue in her pocket.

She broke up the party so they could be home by the time an occupational therapist arrived. Tom looked quite seriously at her mother and said, "I'd be glad to drive you."

"Supposed to walk," Mom told him—minus the first syllable.

Again, he clearly understood and said, "Then let me

walk you two home. You have quite a garden, Mrs. Hendrick. I wish I'd seen it when all those roses were in bloom."

Somehow, he managed to continue gently chattering as Jordan's mother labored along at a snail's pace. He admired the ramp, and suggested they add an arch over it by spring. "With a climbing rose, it'd look like it's been here forever."

They parted at the back door on a cordial note, Jordan relieved when he left with that long, confident and yet slightly stiff stride. Could he possibly be as nice a guy as he seemed?

Jordan was disconcerted by her suspicion. Of course there were decent men out there. That didn't mean she wanted anything to do with one who showed up on her doorstep.

Now all she had to do was listen to Mom talk about what a gentleman he was, and how perhaps they ought to have him over so he and Jordan could get to know each other.

Not a chance. The very fact that she found Tom Moore to be attractive—never mind his *niceness*—punctuated the importance of keeping her distance. Really, that shouldn't be a problem now, with him apparently having started work. He'd soon find friends.

What she should do was quit sitting out on the front porch.

TWICE IN THE next week Tom saw Jordan heading out for a run. The second time he was able to change to sweats and athletic shoes in time to trail some distance behind, waiting until she'd circled to head back to finally catch up with her maybe half a mile from their homes. He didn't mind the hanging back part, given that he had plenty of time to appreciate how good she looked in stretchy women's running pants and top. He'd been right about her build—long, slender legs could give him plenty of fantasies, and he liked the curvaceous hips just as much, although they wouldn't serve a dedicated runner.

They were fine by him.

Once he stepped it up, she heard his approaching footsteps, looked over her shoulder and half tripped before catching her balance. She appeared startled to see him, and not really pleased, but slowed down when he did and asked civilly, "Don't you have to work?" Her face gleamed with sweat, but she wasn't gasping for breath which meant she was in decent condition.

"I'm doing some work remotely." He was intensely relieved to slow from a jog to a walk. He pushed through pain every day but didn't enjoy it. "I'm...not so much the guy you'll see mowing the grass at the park or cleaning the public restrooms." He grinned. "Can't say I mind that. I'm mostly in administration, which means endless reports. The county is like any form of government—they're fond of rules and regulations. I'm acquainting myself with all of them and issues the parks department has had in the past as well as ideas for expansion." He paused, glancing out of the corner of his eye at her. "I'll be called out for any public disturbances or crimes, too. If you see me carrying a weapon, that's why."

"Oh." She didn't look at him. Had she just slotted him into place with the cops who were making her life miserable?

Officer Wilson and Deputy Chief Bowen, recognizable to Tom from photos, had stopped by together twice this week, keeping the pressure on but learning nothing new. Tom had no idea how much Jordan's mother knew. He hoped not much.

"If my truck is in the driveway and you want company on a run, give me call," he suggested. "In fact, how about

I give you my phone number in case you need a hand with your mother?"

Her glance struck him as suspicious, but she took out her phone and entered his number. She had to know that if her mother took a fall in the middle of the night, say, he could get there quicker than anyone else.

They parted ways, Tom smiling, Jordan merely nodding. He'd believed he'd made some inroads the other day, when she and her mother visited, but Jordan must have been faking it for her mother's sake.

This was his investigation now, but the department was pretending he didn't exist. He was working remotely, all right, reading every scrap of information he could find about her.

Yesterday, he'd killed hours researching violent crimes that occurred in Great Falls, Montana, during the couple of years she'd lived there. A city of over 60,000 people, Great Falls was impacted by a lot more tourism than he'd have suspected given the distance from Yellowstone to the south and Glacier National Park to the northwest. The police department and county sheriff's department stayed plenty busy, he determined, but he also hadn't hit on any murder or violent assault that jumped out at him. He might circle back later, but had decided to take a look at the couple of years she'd stayed here in Storm Lake before moving away, and her first year in Walla Walla and then the two-year gap between the deaths of the two men so far linked to her. He assumed the Walla Walla investigators were doing the same, but he preferred to do his own research. In fact, he felt some uneasiness about the competence of his new department.

Call him credulous, but he was having trouble envisioning her as a killer. He kept seeing patience and tenderness with her mother. The small touches that spoke louder than words. He'd felt some tightening in his chest that was unfamiliar.

He was also perplexed as to how to build trust between himself and Jordan. She was conspicuously *not* hanging out on the front porch anymore. Four days after the cookie delivery, he succeeded in setting out on a run only minutes behind her, but when he caught up, she came right out and said, "If you don't mind, I like running alone." After a pause, she did make an effort to soften the rejection. "It's the one time my mind can free float."

"I understand that." That might even be true, but he suspected that wasn't why she'd slapped him down. "See you," he added, and turned on the afterburners to leave her behind.

When he passed a small neighborhood park, he turned to round the block it occupied and saw Jordan continue on ahead. Probably running to the lakeshore and maybe a distance beyond it. The minute she was out of sight, he slowed to a walk and bent over with his hands on his hips.

Damn, damn, *damn*. He felt as if his left femur had snapped—again.

Walk it off, he told himself, and did. He chose a route that wouldn't intersect with Jordan's and finally was able to ease into a jog again. Yeah, he definitely wasn't ready to run a perp down, unless it was a six-year-old who'd just lifted a candy bar from a convenience store.

The chagrin he felt for the slowness of his physical recovery might be the cake, but Jordan Hendrick had supplied the icing. His ego insisted her attitude had nothing to do with *him*, and everything to do with her predicament. Unfortunately, he couldn't be sure.

He'd gotten home and showered before he saw her walk

into sight and head up to the front door. A minute later, a smiling fellow came out, lifted a hand and left in a sedan parked in the driveway. He looked familiar and was presumably one of the aides or therapists that came and went.

Tom brooded. Maybe this wasn't going to work. So far as he could see, the pressure the cops were applying wasn't working, either. She was a strong woman. So strong, he'd like to know what had happened in her brief marriage.

He'd read the reports from first responders, including the eventual interviews with her, and he'd seen the photographs. The one of her brutally battered face sickened him. He reminded himself that she had only been nineteen and in the marriage for a year and a half. Teenagers weren't famous for common sense. Hadn't she felt she could turn to her mother?

He didn't think it'd go well if he dropped by and asked, "Hey, can we talk about your marriage? Didn't end so well, did it?"

To cap an unsuccessful week, he was out in front raking up what he hoped were the last leaves from that enormous maple when a police car pulled into her driveway. The front door of the house opened, and Jordan stepped out. She looked straight at him, and for a long moment that look held. He couldn't be sure from this distance but thought her cheeks reddened. She turned to Officer Wilson and didn't let herself so much as glance at Tom again.

Damn. Now she knew he knew if he hadn't already. Unless he pretended to worry and knocked on her door later to ask what was up, and imply he'd be glad to listen?

That little fantasy lasted about five seconds. She'd hold her chin high and say, "This doesn't concern you," followed by, "No, thanks."

What he'd do was keep investigating without talking to

her. He'd spoken once with a Walla Walla detective. Since then, he had thought of additional questions. Surely it had occurred to those investigators that, if she were a killer, there might be other victims?

So far, he hadn't dared talk to anyone here in town, in case his name got back to Jordan. He was itching, though, to get a better idea why she didn't seem to have friends who welcomed her back to town. There might have been red flags about her personality all along that had been ignored. And what about her dead husband's friends and family? He bet they could give him an earful. As it was, the only relatives he knew about for sure were the mother, sister and brother. Small town like this, there might be others.

For now, he'd keep his cover here in Storm Lake. With time, Jordan might soften. Given the apparent lack of friends, if she were innocent, wouldn't she be desperate for someone to listen, to maybe believe in her?

Here he was, ready and waiting to be that guy.

WHAT DIFFERENCE DID it make that Tom Moore must now know what police suspected about her? She hated the humiliation that washed over her when he saw the cops arrive and his eyes widened. It wasn't as if he was anything more to her than a new neighbor who disturbed her for reasons she refused to analyze. So what if he immediately concluded he'd associated with one of the rare female serial killers?

The police were leaning hard, but it hadn't occurred to Chief Guthrie that including the deputy chief would just get her back up. Wilson was too young to have been around then, but knowing Bowen could have been in a position to see her unconscious and battered made her skin crawl now. Plus, Steve had really liked the man, who had stepped in some once Steve's dad died. They'd gone hunting together but took their trophies to Steve's mother instead of Jordan, who couldn't have dealt with a dead deer or a wild turkey complete with feathers. Of course, that was a small town for you. She knew several other of the officers from school, or because she'd gone to school with their kids.

In the next week, she tried harder not to notice Tom when he set out for a run or washed that big black SUV in his driveway even though it already looked shiny to her. She should probably do the same to her mother's car, and hers, but that would leave her exposed out front, where anyone could see her and wander over for a friendly conversation.

Better not.

Mom had become more time-consuming, not less, as she became more active, her natural determination and stubbornness surfacing. She became testy when Jordan hovered. She had enough of that from the therapists and the aide who still didn't think she should shower by herself. She could handle enough tasks now, she thought she ought to be unsupervised while she did so. Jordan could only be grateful that November had brought plunging temperatures. If it had been high summer, Mom would have insisted on working in the garden, and just try to stop her! As it was, she watched like a hawk while Jordan planted bulbs, handing out a few at a time because only *she* knew what she wanted where.

Mom's garden, she reminded herself. *Not mine.*

Mom didn't like the row of pillows that kept her from rolling out of bed, either.

"I feel like I'm in a crib," she complained.

Increasingly, Jordan found she'd kicked a couple of them onto the floor by morning. Mom was getting stronger by the day now, but slowly, not by great leaps. Jordan understood her frustration. She'd started demanding to see the bills, too, and didn't appreciate having them withheld. *If anything was likely to give her another stroke*, Jordan thought, but really, Mom's insurance had covered a surprising amount.

Even so, Jordan was starting to think it might be a good idea for her to find a job. Mom wouldn't be going back to work anytime soon, and one of them should bring in some income. Oh, no—at what point would Mom lose her health insurance?

Thank God she owned the house outright.

Jordan had barely fallen asleep one night after her usual hour-plus of worrying when she snapped awake again. What…?

She frowned at the darkness. Mom hadn't cried out. No, she'd heard a thud. Something hitting the side of the house, or someone falling.

Pulse accelerating, she leaped from bed, stumbled over the rug and regained her balance before she reached the hall. If it was Mom, she hadn't turned on a light. Jordan switched on the light in the hall. She immediately saw her mother's bare feet and legs lying on the floor just inside the bathroom.

"Mom! Oh my God, what happened?" She rushed forward to see her mother lying on her side, absolutely still on the bathroom floor. Blood ran over her face and darkened her newly washed and styled hair.

It was all Jordan could do to straddle her mother's body— no, no, to straddle her *mother*—and to search for a pulse. For a frightening minute, she couldn't find one, but then did. It seemed…steady, but her mother was unconscious.

Had she had another stroke? Or overestimated her strength and fallen? It appeared she'd bashed her head against the toilet going down.

911.

Jordan scrambled backward and raced into her room, snatching up her phone and dialing with a shaking hand. The woman she spoke to projected calm.

"If you'd like to stay on the line…"

"No." Tom. He'd come. However resistant she'd been to him, she knew he'd come.

He answered on the third ring, voice muzzy.

"My mother fell… Or…I'm not sure. This is Jordan," she remembered to explain. "Across the street. I…actually don't know why I'm calling you."

"Have you called 911?" Was that clothing rustling in the background?

"Yes." Tears seeped from her eyes. "I'm sorry. I shouldn't have—"

Any vestige of sleep had left his deep voice. "I'm on my way."

He ended the call. Jordan hurried to stand by her mother's feet, then realized she'd have to let the medics in anyway, so she raced to the front door and flipped the dead bolt just as a knock hammered on the door. She flung it open, and Tom stepped in.

The next instant, his arms were around her and he gave her a hard hug that was immensely reassuring for no reason she could determine.

Because someone else is here, she decided. *I'm not alone.*

"Down the hall?" he asked, and she nodded.

Without another word, he moved fast. Jordan left the front door wide open despite the cold air rushing in and followed. She found him crouched in the bathroom, obviously taking Mom's pulse with his fingertips. He abandoned that to gently probe her head. He must have some medical training. Maybe that was a requirement for people working in parks.

Seeing Jordan, he said, "She's definitely developing a bump. Until she wakes up, there's no way to determine whether she just got too ambitious and fell, or whether she had an attack of dizziness, or—"

"Another stroke," she said dully.

She'd been hearing a siren, she realized, which grew in volume. Within minutes someone rapped on the open door. "Hello?"

"Back here," Tom called, and feet sounded on the steps.

Jordan retreated out of the way. When the pair of EMTs or paramedics or whatever they were came in sight carrying packs of equipment and a backboard, she stepped into a bedroom.

"It's my mom. She's been recovering from a stroke. I don't know what happened. She's supposed to ring a bell if she needs to get up in the middle of the night."

"All right."

Tom stepped out of their way and went right to Jordan's side. She didn't resist when he wrapped an arm securely around her again, or when after a few minutes he said, "We'll want to follow them to the hospital. Why don't you get dressed?"

She looked down at herself wearing a sacky T-shirt and faded flannel pajama pants. At any other time, she'd have been embarrassed. As it was, she snuffled and backed away. "Yes. Of course. Thank you."

The medics took her mother out with stunning speed. Jordan had barely donned jeans and a sweatshirt when they passed in the hall. Mom looked so frail Jordan's fear ratcheted up.

She heard Tom saying something about them being right

behind the ambulance. She pulled on socks and thrust her feet into a pair of boots she could zip, then rushed to the living room.

The siren still wailed when she reached the front porch where Tom waited. Lights on the rear of the ambulance receded. Neighbors had come out on their porches, but she couldn't acknowledge them.

"Wait," she said. "I have to get Mom's wallet with her insurance card." Her own bag with her keys, too.

She found both quickly. Still on her porch, Tom displayed no sign of impatience. "Let me drive," he said. "You shouldn't when you're so rattled."

Oh, heavens—he sounded like Detective Shannon. He was right, though. In retrospect, she didn't know how she'd made it so many miles home with her thoughts racing and only a couple of phone updates to let her know that her mother was still alive.

Now…she tried to calm herself. "I can make it on my own," she said. "I'm…okay. But… I'm really glad you came. Thank you."

Those blue eyes never left her face. "You're welcome. I'm not letting you do this alone, either."

"You hardly know us," she argued, even as he watched while she locked the door, then hustled her across the street.

He simply bundled her into the passenger side of his massive vehicle without bothering to argue. The engine roared to life, and she huddled there, grateful. So grateful.

Chapter Seven

In the excruciating hours that followed, Tom barely left her side. His presence felt...surreal. Who was he? Why was he here? He couldn't possibly *want* to be. Could he?

And yet, at some point, she realized he was a sturdy bulwark she'd never had before. Not once did she see so much as a flicker of discomfort in his eyes. For a stranger, he had a remarkable ability to figure out what she needed before she did.

Most of the time, they sat side by side on chairs in the waiting room. His feet stayed square on the floor. He didn't fidget the way she did. When he moved, it was to get her a cup of coffee, or to lay a strong arm around her shoulders when he guessed she was close to shattering.

A doctor or nurse appeared a few times to pull down a mask and give them an update.

"We don't believe she had another stroke," was the first and most heartening.

"Our worry is that she could have broken a hip."

Oh God; something else to terrify her. Recovering from a broken hip could take months that would set Mom's recovery back immeasurably.

"No broken bones," was the next report, "but she hasn't regained consciousness. We'll do an MRI as soon as the staff get in."

Regional hospital or not, it wasn't huge. They probably didn't need MRIs run in the middle of the night very often.

Nodding her understanding, Jordan felt herself sag. This time, when Tom wrapped her in a reassuring embrace, she let herself lean into him and shed a few tears against his sturdy shoulder. What would she have done without him?

Called one of Mom's friends, she supposed. Bonnie would have come in a heartbeat, for example, but she'd have needed to talk and talk…and a hug from her wouldn't have been the same.

Maybe, Jordan thought, she'd isolated herself from old friends more than she needed to. The thing was, their lives had moved on, and she'd been conscious of how little they had in common with her on those occasions she'd encountered one or the other at the grocery store or post office.

She could just hear herself say, *You haven't been interviewed by a police detective? Why, you haven't lived until that happens!*

Plus, she bet the few female friends who weren't married could go out with a guy they'd met as many times as they wanted without condemning him to death.

Speaking of police…she wondered why Tom hadn't asked about the cops he'd seen on her doorstep. Or did he already know from neighbors or people at work?

More people filtered into the waiting room when morning arrived. Jordan kept a wary eye out for anyone who looked familiar. What if Steve's mother had some health blip and Kevin brought her to the ER? Oh, Lord—she'd been lucky not to see either of them so far. Of course, that would be because she left the house only to accomplish essential errands, and to drive Mom for checkups and tests here at the hospital.

And to run. But why would Kevin Dunn be in her neighborhood by happenstance to see her go by? One thing she had done when she first came home was look him up to be sure he didn't live nearby.

Unless he knew she was home and was keeping an eye on her? Creepy thought. He and his mother and plenty of Steve's friends had made it known that they believed Jordan had murdered her husband, who would never have attacked her. Not the sainted Steve Dunn.

She sighed, made herself straighten, and went back to staring at the closed double doors she had yet to be allowed to go through.

TOM HAD FORGOTTEN he was a cop, far less a detective investigating this woman, from the minute her call had pulled him from sleep. He had hated hearing how frantic she was. Given that he had medical training to deal with many emergencies, he'd shot out of bed and across the street. Seeing fear in those warm brown eyes that had to be genuine, he wouldn't have left Jordan's side even if their acquaintance was as casual as she believed it to be. She needed someone, and he found he didn't at all mind being that person.

She smelled good. Shampoo, maybe, but he liked the sweetness. He'd come close to burying his face in her hair several times during the night. He liked her slender bone structure, the generous breasts he was careful not to inadvertently glance at, and the strength that ensured every time a medical professional appeared, she sat or stood straight up on her own.

He wondered if she questioned her decision to trust him this far.

They'd sat together in near silence for a lot of hours when she turned those troubled eyes on him and asked, "Are your parents alive?"

He hesitated long enough for her to say, "It's none of my business. You don't have to—"

He interrupted. "I don't know."

Her eyes widened. "How can you not know?"

"I grew up in the foster care system. There are plenty of us in this country who did."

"But…weren't you told about, I don't know, your mother at least?"

"They guessed she was a teenager who couldn't keep me. I was dropped at a fire station. Since I was obviously premature, I had to stay in the hospital for a couple of months. There were concerns that I'd have ongoing health issues, which kept me from appealing to adoptive parents who wanted a baby."

Her mouth fell open. "That stinks!"

She wasn't thinking of her mother now. Maybe that's why he forced himself to go on, talk about something he usually kept to himself.

His mouth twitched in a half smile at her vehemence. "You're right. It does. I also understand. When people have a child with problems, they usually deal. Taking on one that isn't yours is different."

Jordan snorted.

He laughed. "It wasn't that bad. After a few short placements, I ended up in a really solid foster home for years until my foster dad had an early heart attack. One of those things where he just dropped dead on an outdoor basketball court where he was playing a pickup game. There was a flaw in his heart, and it kicked in."

Her gaze hadn't once left his since he started talking. "How old were you?"

Had she even blinked?

"Twelve."

"Oh." She seemed to wrench her gaze away at last. The pause drew on long enough, Tom began to think it was up to him to fill it, but then she said, "That's how old I was when my parents got divorced."

"Tough age."

"Is any age good to lose your father?" Anger and something else infused her voice.

The background info he was given hadn't mentioned her father. Now he wondered whether that gap didn't hold critical insights into her psychology.

She shook herself. "Oh, I don't know why I started this conversation."

"Hey, what else do we have to do?" He managed a wry smile. "It's...natural to think about your parents when one of them is in the hospital." The way his foster father died, he'd only attended the funeral. "Did you keep seeing your father?"

"No. I never saw him again, and he didn't even really say goodbye." She was back to staring at the doors into the ER, but probably wasn't actually seeing them. "I...grieved for a long time. I built him up into something he never was. It took me forever to admit that he hadn't been that great a parent." She shrugged. "He became a long-haul truck driver, which meant he was gone a lot. That would have been okay if he'd been more *present* when he was home, but he tended to drink a lot of beer and watch sports. Maybe it was different when I was younger, but...I don't remember. I'm pretty sure he wasn't much of a husband, either. I guess one day he just announced he could find a better berth between hauls and walked out."

She did turn her head then, and the pain in her eyes was very apparent. "Mom never faltered, and I always knew it was for *me*. I know how lucky I was. Because...because she tried so hard, I felt protective of her, too. You know?"

Tom didn't say anything—platitudes wouldn't help—but he took her hand and held on. That was one question answered. She could well have felt she had to hide the problems in her marriage from her mother.

"I can't lose her." Her eyes swam with tears for only the second time of the night. "I can't."

"Hey." He bent far enough to kiss the top of her head. "Here's the doctor again."

"Oh, God." Jordan swiped frantically at the tears and straightened. "Dr. Pratt?"

This time, the middle-aged woman was smiling. Jordan shot to her feet, but the doctor came to them and sank down in a chair.

"I'm glad to say, your mother has regained consciousness. Aside from the concussion itself, she has a headache and some bruises, but that's all. We want to keep her for at least another twenty-four hours, but you can come back and see her now if you'd like."

"Please." Jordan quivered like a deer in that second before it sprang away.

Weariness on her face, the doctor laughed. "Only you," she warned, and Tom nodded his understanding.

Jordan whirled to face him. "I should have thought of this. If you want to go home, I can—"

"No, Jordan." He took her hand again and squeezed. "I don't mind waiting. Take your time."

The shimmer of tears in her beautiful eyes gave him a kick in his chest. Damn, he had to watch this. If she found out—no, *when* she found out—there'd be no forgiveness, even though tonight hadn't been about his job at all.

Uh-huh. He hadn't volunteered information on his own background just so she'd open up about her own? That wasn't about the job?

Weirdly, he wasn't sure it had been, but she wouldn't believe that, would she?

He felt a little sick as he watched her walk away and disappear through those doors.

JORDAN WALKED ALONG when her mother was moved upstairs to a room. She'd gotten used to the physical damage from the stroke, but now her awareness of Mom's fragility shook her.

She tried to hide that. When her mother grabbed her hand—the one Tom had held for so much of the night—and said in that slurred voice, "I was so silly! All I did was make more trouble. I'm so sorry!"

"You have no reason to be sorry," Jordan said sternly. "I don't want to hear it. You're a smart woman who thought she could do something as simple as go to the bathroom by herself. You just haven't adjusted to your muscle loss. And with the help of all those evil therapists working you so hard, you'll regain your strength before you know it."

"If I just hadn't worn my slippers. One of them got tangled up, and…"

Jordan vaguely recalled seeing a slipper lying in the hall. The other must be in the bathroom. "How about we buy you a new pair that aren't so floppy?"

A sound startlingly like a giggle came out of her mother. "*I'm* floppy!"

A laugh burst out, and the two of them kept laughing long enough to let go of some of the awful tension.

Mom settled down after that and was asleep within minutes. Jordan sat there for another twenty minutes, but she felt guilty about leaving Tom waiting, and anyway… She was exhausted.

She slipped out in the hall and told the nurse who'd

settled her mother that she was going home for a nap but would be back this afternoon.

Then she went back downstairs and found Tom in the same chair, seemingly engrossed reading something on his phone. When he heard her footsteps, though, he looked up with a smile.

"Everything okay?"

"Yes!" Then she made a face. "Except I need a nap."

"You and me both." His grin presumably wasn't intended to be sexy, but she couldn't help noticing the way it deepened a crease in one cheek and flashed even white teeth. Foster kid or not, he'd obviously had excellent dental and orthodontic care.

Or had been born with perfect teeth.

She had to be giddy.

The daylight startled her when they got outside. He rested a hand on her back as they walked out to where he'd left his truck in the parking lot. She noticed the contact, but it felt normal after the last twelve hours when he'd been touching her much of the time.

His hand *almost* touched her butt when he boosted her up into the passenger seat before slamming the door.

When he got in, she said, "Why do you drive something so humungous?"

His sidelong grin was even sexier, if that was possible. "Because I like big trucks?"

She blew a raspberry.

He laughed. "I bought it new after I accepted the job here. It seemed sensible for hard winters. Looks like a fair amount of snowfall is the norm."

He was right. She should upgrade her tires.

Warm air barely had time to start blowing before they pulled up to the curb in front of her house. He turned off the engine as she reached for the door handle but turned to face him.

"I don't know how to begin to thank you."

He shook his head. "I'll walk you to your door."

"You don't need—"

He hopped out before she could finish her sentence and circled around to meet her. "Feeling better?"

"Yes!" She was going to crash anytime, she knew she was, but right now she buzzed with giddy energy. "I want to dance!" A tune came to her, and she started to hum "I Could Have Danced All Night," from *My Fair Lady*. She didn't remember the rest of the lyrics, but she held out her arms as if she had a partner and began to twirl across the driveway.

To her astonishment, Tom bowed formally and held out a hand. "May I have this dance?"

Laughing, she laid her hand in his, and they began to waltz, albeit in a very confined space. Only for a few minutes, but her heart had swelled by the time they slowed, and he smiled down ather.

"You can waltz."

"Took ballroom dance in college." This smile was more wry. "To impress a girl, of course. Haven't done it since."

"Most people our age don't." Wow. She had to blink to bring the world into focus. "Thank you again. I think I need to lie down."

He ushered her to her front door, kissed her forehead and gently pushed her inside.

She was crossing the kitchen when it occurred to her the front door hadn't been locked. No wonder, in the frenzy of getting out of here. She did lock it behind her, thinking only about her bed...until she saw it. She froze in the doorway, staring. The covers were pulled invitingly back…and a butcher knife lay on the pillow.

She rushed to search the house, including her old bedroom upstairs. Once sure she was alone, she fell to her knees in front of the toilet and surrendered to the nausea.

Afterward, she considered photographing the scene, but what was the point? She could so easily have set this up herself, who would believe her? So she returned the knife to its place in a drawer in the kitchen, changed the sheets, dragged a chair from the dining room to brace her room door, and fell into bed. She'd think about this later.

Along with the fact that anyone at all could have seen her dancing on the driveway with her handsome neighbor. How could she have been so careless?

TOM MANAGED TO sleep for a few hours, but was awake to watch from his front window when, midafternoon, Jordan drove away, presumably to the hospital. A part of him wished he was going with her, but of course that was ridiculous. Unwise, too. He'd felt more for her since that middle-of-the-night call than he could afford. It wasn't like him to feel these stirrings.

Black widow, remember? Lures men into her web, then kills them.

He believed that was true even less than he had before. That said, he couldn't forget that plenty of general scumbags—*and* killers—also loved someone. Jordan obviously didn't blame her mother in any way for what happened with the husband, so her loyalty remained solid.

Last night, the cop in him had briefly wondered whether she might have gotten tired of taking care of her mother. The scene hadn't supported anything like that. Mom's only injury, as it turned out, was the blow to the head, which had clearly been from contact with the toilet. Not a very sure way to knock anyone off, and the risk was there that her mother would wake up exclaiming that she'd been pushed. Jordan had to know eyes would turn her way.

Plus, Jordan had called him and let him see her fear.

She couldn't be that good an actor, could she?

Damn, Tom hated knowing how she'd feel if she learned he had even briefly suspected something like that.

Circling back to the marriage, Tom might have doubted that the husband—Steve Dunn—was abusive, except that about six months before the blowup when she shot the guy, he'd taken her to an emergency room. Not here in town; he'd driven her a ridiculous distance to a hospital across the state line into Washington, presumably not wanting anyone who knew either of them to see her. The injuries were classic: spiral fracture of both lower arm bones on the left side—typically caused by violently twisting the forearm—along with a broken collarbone on the right side of her body as well as bruises and a burst eardrum. There had to have been bruises. It would have taken quite a blow to burst the eardrum.

Even if Jordan had lied to protect her husband, how had nobody asked serious questions and red-flagged the visit? As a patrol officer and detective, Tom had dealt with enough domestic violence to recognize the particular injuries.

Thinking about the complex, damaged woman he was getting to know, he had a feeling that any man who tried to lay his hands on her that way now would be deeply sorry. He was also beginning to understand why she'd been susceptible to abuse at such a young age.

Father walked when she was on the cusp of womanhood, probably leaving her lacking some confidence. Handsome,

popular guy wants *her*—of course she'd be dazzled. Then
the slow progression to turn her into an abused wife—a slap,
a blow, apologies and even gifts, a teenage Jordan dazed
enough to wonder if it all wasn't her fault.

What she'd said tonight had given him a clue about why
she hadn't left the guy early on and gone home to mommy.
Pride, first. Who wanted to make their first big decision as
an adult and have to admit within months that it had been
a whopping mistake? But worse, in her case: she wanted to
protect her mother from upsetting news. She'd likely been
afraid her mother would blame herself because of her own
failed marriage and the impact it had had on her child. No,
Jordan had told herself she could deal with it—and maybe
she'd even believed that, if good ol' Steve was still apolo-
gizing and doing his best to convince her that theirs was a
love match, he'd just been under a lot of stress, it wouldn't
happen again.

By the book.

Unless, Tom thought, *I'm fooling myself because I* like
the woman.

Entirely too much.

Yeah, her marriage had been a disaster, but it sounded
as if she'd given the man she'd initially loved every chance.
Tom's reaction to that was complicated, given that he'd
spent a lifetime wondering why his biological mother hadn't
made even the smallest effort to keep him.

He was usually good at detachment, necessary for a homicide detective and coming naturally to a kid who'd been
tossed around in the foster care system. If he'd ever needed
it, it was now.

He had to reserve judgment. Investigate, instead of trusting what information he'd been given. Try to draw Jordan
in, sure, but only because he was undercover for that ex-

press purpose. Any kind of relationship would not end well, no matter how his investigation turned out, but he couldn't worry about that. Instead, he'd take ruthless advantage of the opening her mother's fall had given him.

He'd start with a call this evening, a simple *How's she doing?* Couldn't go wrong with that.

He shook off the memory of sweeping Jordan around in a briefly magical dance and paced off some of his restlessness. Time for some PT, he decided, including weights. A dose of pain and suffering might get his head in the right place, too.

Chapter Eight

Jordan had never fallen into friendship so fast. She wouldn't even let herself *think* that it might be more. Unless and until the police, here or in Walla Walla, arrested a killer, she could never *have* more. She wasn't even sure she was capable of more.

Yet Tom was just *there* when she wanted to talk. After Mom's doctors decided to keep her a second night, he insisted on coming with Jordan to pick her up the next morning—although they took her car, given the height disadvantage of his SUV.

Jordan hovered closer to home for a few days, but once the awful bruise on her mother's face began to fade and she insisted the headache was gone, running seemed like a good option to de-stress and get out of the house. She hesitated the first time, but it would be rude not to call Tom and find out if he wanted to come, wouldn't it? Honestly, she was surprised he was home—he seemed to work remotely most of the time—but, after all, an increasing number of Americans did work remotely these days.

She'd actually looked up the parks and recreation department to find there were a whole lot more parks than she'd realized, including trails, picnic grounds and ball fields. The rangers apparently had the power to issue anything from a ticket to taking someone in custody for a misdemeanor offense. Who knew? She didn't see his name listed, but the site probably hadn't been updated recently.

The air was crisp and cold when the two of them set out. Their breaths puffed out in clouds. It seemed to her he was moving with less stiffness, although she could tell he hurt by the time they got back to their block. Whether it was true or not, Tom insisted doctors and physical therapists assured him that running was a good exercise unless he pushed it to the point of excessive pain.

"Oh, I've had plenty of PT," he said ruefully. "Your mom and I have more in common than she knows."

After all he'd done, it seemed only decent to invite him to dinner.

As they trotted to a stop mid-street between their houses, he gave her a surprised glance.

"You sure? I don't want to make more work for you."

"I cook every night. I won't guarantee fine dining."

His devastating grin came close to buckling her knees given their already weakened state. "I'm not a fancy guy."

"But you know how to waltz," Jordan teased.

He laughed as he walked away.

She'd never tell him that she'd put more effort into the meal than she did on an average day. Mom ate like a bird, so cooking for her benefit wasn't very satisfying.

Jordan felt uneasy when she watched Tom approach from across the street and come up to the front porch even though there was no reason anyone would think he was here for her. Whoever hated her so much couldn't be watching *all* the time, and neighbors had always come by this house even before Mom's stroke.

Unless they'd also seen him running with her.

We're not dating, she told herself firmly, and let him in before he even had time to ring the doorbell.

She felt as if she were in a lull—maybe the eye of the hurricane would be a better analogy. Every time she opened the mailbox, she expected to find a rattlesnake coiled and ready to strike, but nothing threatening came. Until the knife, the helium balloon was the last suggestion someone was watching her, and that had been months ago. If she hadn't so carelessly left the front door unlocked, she wanted to think the knife thing wouldn't have happened. Was her enemy mostly satisfied because, once again, the police suspected her of a murder? But so far, the investigation seemed to have stalled, probably because there was no physical evidence to connect her to the crime, just as there'd been none back in Walla Walla.

What would happen if this murder dwindled into a cold case? Would some guy she'd chatted to briefly at the grocery store be killed?

Or—oh, God, the nice guy who lived across the street from her? The one she'd spent more time with than she had any of the men she'd dated before their deaths?

But she wasn't dating Tom Moore, and she wouldn't. She convinced herself that's what mattered. What relationship she had with him didn't fit the pattern.

Over the course of the week, they ran again together. He showed up unannounced once, tools in hand, to work on the railing framing the front porch steps. He'd noticed one side wasn't quite solid.

"I know your mother goes out the back," he said, "but that'll change." When he was finished, he left without saying anything.

Jordan invited him to dinner again. He was all but offering to let her and Mom, too, lean on him. She owed him.

Plus, he had devoured that first meal, making her suspect he might normally subsist on microwavable meals from the frozen food case at the store.

That evening, Jordan served a spicy vegetarian chili that she and her mother both liked and added corn bread and defrosted home-baked oatmeal and raisin cookies that had come from Mrs. Welsh in the house on the corner.

As they ate, Tom asked Mom about her physical therapy. What she didn't mind doing, what she dreaded.

"Like exercising to make me stronger," her mother said after a moment. Her speech had noticeably become clearer, but so slowly Jordan was surprised in that moment at how easy she was to understand.

Certainly Tom understood her, because he nodded. "I felt that way, too, even if it hurts sometimes."

"What…happened to you?" Mom asked.

Would he answer?

His hesitation was noticeable, but finally he said, "I was shot. Multiple times." Seeing their expressions, he grimaced. "Yes, it happens to park rangers occasionally, too, especially in a big city. I approached a guy we'd been keeping an eye on. He didn't want to talk. He opened fire instead." His voice thickened. "A friend was killed, too."

Another ranger, presumably.

Her mother lifted a shaky hand and reached out farther than Jordan had known she could with her weak arm. She laid the hand on Tom's arm. He looked down, up quickly at Jordan, letting her see how moved he was, then pressed his own hand over her mother's.

"Thank you," he said quietly, that deep resonance in his voice giving Jordan goose bumps.

Once everyone had time to take a couple more bites, he

smiled at her mother. "We got sidetracked. Which PT do you like least?"

This answer required Jordan to translate, although she tried not to make it obvious that's what she was doing. "Occupational and sometimes speech? I didn't know that, Mom."

Her mother's frustration trying to explain distressed Jordan and, she thought, Tom, but the gist became clear. Therapists often assumed she didn't know *how* to do something, when in fact she did. She just *couldn't* do it because of limited physical ability. "I'm not a child."

When Jordan walked Tom to the front door, she said, "I know I keep thanking you, but I have to do it again. I never thought to ask whether she felt all her PT was useful. I'm glad you got her talking."

"There may still be reasons why her doctor will insist they keep on," he warned.

"But at least I know to talk to them." She lifted a hand and realized in horror she wanted to lay it on his chest. Curling her fingers, she snatched the hand back.

His eyebrows rose, and there was a peculiar pause, the kind where oxygen seemed to be lacking. It must be the way he was looking at her, his blue eyes so intent she had to fight the desire to sway toward him.

No, no, no! She couldn't afford a complication like this. They were becoming friends, that's all.

Suddenly, he shuttered his expression. "Good night, Jordan," he said in a low rumble, and let himself out.

She hustled to the window and watched him cross the street in reverse, his passage obvious thanks to the light at the corner.

For a second time in a matter of minutes, the very air

seemed to be stolen from her. What if somebody had let themselves into his house and was waiting?

Her rib cage tightened. She should back off. Make it coolly apparent she and Mom didn't need him.

Only, she hadn't felt alone this past week the way she had for so many years. She'd never tell him that; it would be completely normal for him to make friends through work, start seeing a woman, and as Mom regained her normal capabilities, do little more than wave at her or Jordan when he saw them coming or going.

Would it be so bad to soak in his strength and calm good nature while he offered it?

CHIEF GUTHRIE WAS of the opinion that the recent lack of the kind of threats Jordan had claimed she'd gotten previously made it pretty plain she'd made them up…or was responsible for them herself. Otherwise, why nothing since the helium balloon, which she'd destroyed and thrown away without giving a single thought to saving it to show police?

"If she has a stalker, he or she could be satisfied by the intense scrutiny Ms. Hendrick has been under after the latest murder," Tom suggested in their latest face-to-face. He'd have preferred not to chance ever being seen with the police chief, but Guthrie liked a more concrete connection.

Now pulling out his wallet to pay for the lunch they had shared at a hole-in-the-wall café, the chief grunted his dissatisfaction at Tom's point. "Just don't get soft on her."

Tom raised his eyebrows. "You seem to have made up your mind about her, which is just as dangerous."

Guthrie nodded genially at a constituent as they walked out. Only when they paused before parting in the parking lot did he half complain, "Doesn't seem like you're getting anywhere with this."

"Being undercover has advantages, but also a lot of disadvantages. I can't do any investigation into people from her past who might be targeting her. I've compiled a list from social media and started researching backgrounds, but that's the best I can do. Even if she is the black widow you want to think her, these deaths have occurred several years apart. No, the latest was, what, six months after the killing in Walla Walla? Still a break. What makes you think she's going to change that? It wouldn't be smart, not when she knows you're suspicious. In fact, it might be a good tactic if your investigators appear to be backing off. If we're looking at someone besides Ms. Hendrick, he might be angry that she's not being punished the way he thinks she should be."

Guthrie scowled. "My guys won't like it, though. Everyone hereabouts has an opinion about her. But yeah, fine. They're not learning a damn thing, anyway."

Maybe because there was nothing *to* learn from Jordan? Tom carefully didn't say that. He did question whether anyone had looked into the doctor's background, as would be standard. His murder could be completely unrelated to the assault on Elliott Keefe.

The chief snapped, "Of course we did. You concentrate on the Hendrick woman. Push her a little. Dating a man is the trigger, for her or for someone else. You're ideally situated, just the way we planned."

"And she's wary."

"Tempt her then!" Guthrie walked away.

Irritated, Tom watched him go before going to his own vehicle. *Tempt her.* Damn it, *he* was dangerously tempted by *her.* The identification of the killer aside, the idea of setting himself up to be shot again had a cooling effect every time he thought about doing something as foolish as kissing the woman. What's more, that felt like crossing an ethical line that repelled him.

Growling under his breath, he headed over to his office at the parks department. The one he'd been assigned to maintain his cover, just as everyone who worked there knew to take messages for Head Ranger Moore.

So far, there'd been not one. Even the local newspaper remained unaware of a new hire who didn't actually do anything except spend time on the internet in that otherwise pristine office.

He brooded for a while about the pushback he was getting from the chief. *Everyone hereabouts has an opinion about her.* What did that mean? Had Guthrie included himself? Tom sure wasn't satisfied with what details from the investigation he'd been fed. Or maybe it was more what *hadn't* been done or had been left out of reports. Whatever Guthrie claimed, this department hadn't seriously considered the possibility that Jordan was a secondary victim. Because that meant the killer was a local? One of those people who had "an opinion about her"?

He didn't see Jordan or her mother that evening, although he kept an eye on the lights in their house. When he'd first moved in here, he hadn't thought there was a chance in hell that Shelly Hendrick had any chance of truly recovering from what had clearly been a devastating stroke. Now, he was impressed by her. Inspired, too; he knew how hard she had to be working, how discouragement must feel like a high wall in front of her, one she had to knock down brick by brick. She was a gutsy woman, he'd concluded—as was her daughter.

He was always an early riser no matter what time he'd gone to bed. Tom made a habit of starting his mornings with coffee—and, these days, a look out the window at the Hendricks' house. He didn't know what he expected to see—A moving truck backed into the driveway? An ambulance? Fire bursting from every window?—but he had a growing sense of disquiet where his investigation was concerned.

Did he just *want* to believe she was the victim, not the killer? Max had always accused him of being too soft on women. Was it true? Tom would have given a lot to be able to toss around ideas about this investigation with Max.

Growling under his breath, Tom carried his first cup of coffee and strolled into the living room where he had the best view of the houses across the street.

The kitchen was at the back of the Hendrick house, so if the light was on, he couldn't tell. Jordan typically seemed to get up mornings as early as he did. Otherwise... He frowned.

There was...something on the front window. And the garage door?

He set down the mug on a side table, let himself out of his house and trotted at a slant toward Jordan's. He didn't like not carrying, but his cover wouldn't last long if he always wore a shoulder or ankle holster. The back of his neck prickling, he wasn't halfway when he made out the addition to the garage door: spray-painted in bloodred, all in capital letters, the single word *KILLER*.

Swearing, he switched his gaze to the glass of the front window. Smaller of necessity, *KILLER* was spray-painted there, too.

And then he saw the same word sprayed on the driver's-side window of Jordan's car.

He took the steps two at a time, pausing only long enough to touch the paint and determine that it wasn't going to wipe off easily, before he knocked lightly on the door. He hoped Jordan's mother was still asleep. Quiet footsteps approached, there was a pause while Jordan likely checked on who the visitor was through the peephole, and she opened the door.

"Tom?"

He ignored the momentary hit the first sight of her often gave him. He especially liked seeing her first thing in the morning, when she looked less closed up, softer, as if she hadn't donned her armor.

"You need to come out here," he said grimly.

Those caramel-brown eyes widened. "What…?" But she didn't finish the question, instead stepping over the threshold. Her gaze followed the direction of his outstretched hand and she saw the lettering.

"Oh God. Oh God!" She sounded frantic. "I have to clean it off! If people *see* it—"

With her horror so convincing, he hated to say this, but did. "It's on your garage door, too. And your car."

Shoulder brushing him, she ran down the stairs, almost falling on the last two. She was still barefoot, he saw, following her as she ran far enough down the walkway to be able to see both her car and the detached garage.

"Oh God," she said again. "Everybody will see. This will never end!"

"You need to call 911. I don't know what's going on here—" the hell he didn't "—but this is a threat."

Her shoulders sagged as she stared at the two-foot-tall lettering. "Yes. I'll do that." She almost laughed, but without any humor whatsoever. "For what good it'll do."

"You need to get some shoes on, too. It's cold this morning."

Jordan looked down at her feet as if she wasn't sure what he was talking about, then nodded numbly. "I'll have plenty of time before an officer responds."

He could get a faster response for her, but that wouldn't be a good idea. Instead, he walked her back to the porch and said, "I'll circle the house. Make sure the vandal didn't bother with any other surfaces."

A pained sound escaped her as she opened the door. "Thank you."

"Jordan?"

She went still, her back to him.

"You going to explain this to me?"

It was a long moment before her shoulders stiffened again, and she said, "Yes, but…not now."

He made sure he spoke gently. "Okay."

His last glance back saw her on the front porch, phone in hand.

SOMETHING ABOUT THE paint job on her car disturbed her most. The other lettering was sloppy, but this was more deliberately done; one leg of the *K* almost looked like an arrow pointing downward. She was sure she'd locked the car door, she always did, but when she tried it, it opened. Probably she shouldn't be touching the car, but—

Was that her driver's license lying facedown on the floor in front of the gas pedal? How could it be? She bent and picked it up, gave a stifled cry and dropped it. That wasn't *her* license—it was Colin Parnell's. Her teeth chattered. That it was in her car was meant to implicate her further in the murder. And, oh God, it now had her fingerprints on it.

Tom would reappear any minute. *Pocket the license…? No. Push it out of sight under the seat. Lock the door. Close it.*

She had barely done so when she saw the first police unit coming down the street. At least there were no sirens. Jordan had to be grateful for that. She'd asked, but sometimes thought cops all loved drawing as much attention as possible.

Otherwise, Tom determined there was no paint in her garage to cover the writing, so he volunteered to go pick some up, as well as any products he could find that would clean the paint off glass.

While he was gone, it seemed as if every member of the Storm Lake Police Department, from the newest rookie—who'd been the first responder—to Chief Allen Guthrie showed up to take a look. She watched, stiff as a porch upright, scared to death.

Detective Wilson—yes, he'd evidently received his promotion—and Deputy Chief Ronald Bowen finished studying—or were they admiring?—the spray-painting and interrogated her. As always, Wilson sounded almost pleasant, but with a hint of "don't think you're going to fool me" thrown in. The deputy chief balanced him by the contempt overlaid by a veneer of civility. Other people might not notice, but his attitude wasn't much better than Buzz's. She could just imagine the result if she demanded a replacement for him, too.

Jordan responded to questions by rote. No, neither she nor her mother had heard a sound all night. No, she didn't own any cans of spray paint—or cans of any kind of paint, for that matter, unless there were some old ones in the back of the garage. If they found the can of red spray paint, it wouldn't have her fingerprints on it because it wasn't hers.

Detective Wilson asked what she thought the point of the vandalism was. Beside him in the living room, Deputy Chief Bowen raised his eyebrows in challenge.

"Whoever is doing this must be frustrated," she said wearily. "You haven't arrested me. It's a nasty accusation for me, but it's also aimed at you. He clearly thinks he's set me up so well, you're incompetent because you haven't arrested me."

She could tell they didn't like that assessment. If she hadn't hidden the driver's license and locked the car door before they got here, she was chilled to know they'd have had reason to arrest her.

Tom walked into the living room as she finished.

"Mom's in the kitchen," she told him. "The occupational therapist is staying until, well, we're done."

He nodded at her, then at both cops, and went straight through the house toward the kitchen. Thank goodness— Mom was so upset by the events, she was gabbling more than actually speaking, and mad because her tongue wouldn't keep up.

Looking back at the two cops, she said, "I can't tell you anything else. Please let me go to work cleaning and painting."

They glanced at each other. Bowen grunted and heaved his weight to his feet. "I believe we have adequate photographs. Unfortunately, because your driveway and walkway are both paved and the past few days have been dry, there are no visible footprints. We haven't found the spray can, either, which isn't surprising."

She could see in his eyes what he was thinking: because they didn't have a warrant to search the house top to bottom, there were plenty of places she could have hidden an object that size until she saw an opportunity to dispose of it.

Standing to let them out, she felt exhaustion settle down on her as a crushing weight. She even swayed slightly. How much more of this unrelenting suspicion could she bear? It wouldn't stop. Whoever hated her this much wasn't done.

She stood out on the front porch for a moment, watching as the couple of remaining official vehicles drove away.

After she soothed Mom again, she'd do her best to obliterate those messages. Too late, of course. She had no doubt everyone on the block and plenty of passersby, drawn by the police presence, had already seen the accusation everyone knew was aimed at *her*: KILLER.

A hand came to rest on her shoulder. She hadn't heard Tom approaching, but she felt his warmth at her back. He was being supportive...so far.

"I'll take care of the garage if you want to tackle the window," he said.

Even though, when she turned, she saw questions in his eyes, she said, "Thank you for staying."

He only nodded and loped toward the back of his SUV, now parked in her driveway.

Swallowing the lump in her throat, Jordan wondered how much he'd hang around once he heard her story...and got to wondering which parts of it were true.

Chapter Nine

It ranked right up there with the other longest mornings of her life. And gee whiz, they were all ones when police officers had shown up at her door.

When lunchtime rolled around, she found another cause for intense gratitude. Instead of ordering out—Tom must have guessed Mom would have had trouble with pizza—he took the time to make egg salad sandwiches on soft bread in their kitchen and sliced a blueberry cheesecake Mrs. Chung brought over when she came knocking to be sure Mom was okay.

"I don't understand any of this," Mom fretted at the table, although she'd calmed down some. "How could anyone think...?"

Jordan patted her mother's hand. "The police will figure it out, Mom. It's just...a nasty trick."

It occurred to her that *she* was now treating her mother like a child—maybe had been in some ways ever since she came home—but at the moment, she didn't have the energy to do anything else.

She coaxed Mom into lying down for her nap, and sneaked several peeks into the bedroom until she was sure she was asleep. Then Jordan returned to the kitchen, where Tom had efficiently cleaned up and put the remaining cheesecake in the refrigerator.

Hearing her, he turned and met her eyes. "You look like you could use a nap, too."

Her attempt at a smile had to be pitiful. "Except I'd never fall asleep." She wondered if she'd ever again be able to relax into sleep without a care. Who knew what would happen while she was oblivious?

"Why don't we sit in the living room?" he suggested.

She desperately wanted to put this off, but knew she couldn't. Imagine how he'd wonder if she sent him home, then hustled out with a hand vac and dustcloths to frantically clean the *interior* of her car, like that was the most urgent thing she could do. No, no. The police were gone, satisfied for now. Getting the driver's license out of the car and hidden could wait.

She just wished she could forget for a second the knowledge it was sitting there, a trap with sharp teeth.

She took some deep breaths for calm before focusing on the conversation she had to have with Tom. Outside would have been better, but on the front porch they could be seen, and really, it was too cold today to sit and chat outside. So she nodded.

He sank down at one end of the sofa, and after a hesitation, she chose the other end, curling one leg up. The wing chair wasn't all that comfortable, and Mom's upholstered glider...no, it was *hers*.

Tom shifted to better face her. "This isn't really my business."

"You deserve to hear about it. Anyway, you must have heard some of the background."

Gaze steady, he said, "Not enough to put the pieces together."

"*I* don't understand it. It's... I think someone is determined to ruin my life. Only, that person has to be beyond obsessive." She couldn't keep meeting Tom's sharp blue eyes. She looked down at her hands instead. "It has to go back to my marriage. I married right out of high school, even though Mom tried to talk me out of it." Her laugh sounded broken. "Because why wouldn't that be a good idea?"

She skated over the abuse, because she didn't want this man to see her as someone who'd put up with it. Jordan did tell him, briefly, about the disastrous scene where she'd truly believed he would kill her if she didn't kill him first. When she pulled that trigger.

"I was in a coma for twenty-four hours, in the hospital for days. Eventually I learned he'd been fired from his job that day. He...seemed to be in trouble at work a lot. He didn't like to be told what to do, and he had a hair-trigger temper." This laugh wasn't any better. "How could I not know this about him? But I didn't. The thing was, at school, he didn't care much about grades and shrugged off the bad ones, and the football and baseball coaches worshipped at his feet. He really was a talented athlete, but he didn't get recruited by any top colleges. I wonder if they could tell by his grades that he didn't have the discipline they would expect? I don't know. *He* wasn't going to play for some second-tier program that might be willing to take him, so he went to work in construction right out of high school. I don't think he expected the comedown from being admired, girls flirting, guys wanting to hang out with him." She gave a short laugh. "This is a small town. Everyone came to games. I vaguely remember seeing the mayor and most of the members of the police department in the stands, or slapping Steve on the back in congratulations after a game. Everyone wanting to blame *me* for what happened isn't a surprise."

Tom didn't comment, just listened.

She shrugged awkwardly. "Our marriage started great— I thought so, anyway—then went downhill. There was one big blowup, and I was prepared to leave him, but he cried and begged me not to. I had no idea that's the way it goes with men like him. I believed he had it in him to change if I forgave him and stood beside him."

"Did you talk to your mother?"

She blinked away the water in her eyes. "Not the way I should have. In fact…most of it, I didn't tell her. Anyway, not everybody in town was convinced that I had to shoot and kill Steve, even though none of the responding police had any doubt. I was…hurt really badly. But afterward, I'd see these looks. Later, a few people came right out and said hateful things. I tried to avoid running into anyone in Steve's family, or any of his teammates and best buddies. Even with friends, I could see doubt. That's why I finally moved away."

She told him about the couple of years in Montana, getting most of an AA degree but scraping by financially, deciding to try somewhere else and moving to Washington State. "I finished the AA, started taking a few classes with a goal to eventually get a bachelor's degree, and was lucky enough to get on with the post office. The pay let me have a decent place and be able to tell Mom honestly that I was okay and didn't need financial help."

He nodded. She waited for him to ask what she'd majored in, tell her what *he'd* majored in—he had to have a degree for his level of work, didn't he?—but he didn't offer anything.

For an instant, Jordan wondered why she was being so open with him. Chances were good he'd pretend to believe her side but pull away. Why wouldn't he? Everyone else had.

But what was she supposed to do? Say, *See, three men I got involved with were attacked, two are dead, and the police think I did it.*

"I didn't date for years after...you know."

"You didn't trust men?"

"Or myself." She shrugged awkwardly. "Maybe mostly myself. How could I? I married a man who, when he was in a bad mood, thought of me as his punching bag."

Tom's mouth tightened.

"After I moved to Walla Walla—I guess that was the first time I stayed put and didn't apartment hop—I started having some weird stuff happening. Bouquets delivered on the day Steve died. Some creepy cards. I figured Steve's brother or one of his closest friends—maybe even his mother—was holding on to enough anger to need to lash out. It wasn't like they needed to remind me. How could I ever forget that day?"

She waited a little anxiously for his nod of understanding, which comforted her more than it should.

Then she continued, "But a little over three years ago, a nice guy asked me out. I wasn't really attracted to him, but, see, that made him safer. We had two very casual dates. I doubt he'd have suggested we go out again. It was kind of a mutual shrug. Except, three or four days after we had dinner, he apparently walked into his house when some men were stripping it. He was beaten, shot and killed. A detective talked to me a few days later, but briefly. It seemed pretty obvious what happened, although there's never been an arrest."

"So they didn't associate the attack with you."

"There wasn't any reason to. I think there'd been some other similar home robberies. The homeowners just didn't walk into the middle of it. As far as the police were concerned, I was just someone who knew Pete." She sighed. "Maybe a year later, the creep campaign stepped up. Every so often I'd have this feeling someone was watching me. There'd be raps on my windows. The letters and bouquets, of course. My car got keyed. Just enough to keep me on edge."

"I didn't try dating again for three years. Elliott was a Realtor. He started flirting with me when I dropped off mail, and when he asked me out, I thought, why not?" She met Tom's eyes even though he probably saw her desperation. "I'm ashamed to say I wasn't so much interested in him as I wanted to feel *normal*. I was a twenty-eight-year-old woman with hardly any social life."

When the man who'd gone from neighbor to, maybe, best friend so quickly reached out and took her hand in his, she gathered strength from the contact.

"We had dinner once. The next week we took a picnic to the city fireworks display. I'd driven myself, so we parted ways in the parking lot. Next thing I knew, two detectives are on my doorstep. Elliott had gone home and been attacked. Maybe shot first, they're not sure, then beaten. Police think he was left for dead. He was in a coma for days, but he did survive and recover. Unfortunately, he doesn't remember anything that happened. But my name popped up associated with the victim whose attack was similar."

Tom frowned. "Except for the burglary."

"Right." *Get this over with*, she told herself. "The detectives in Walla Walla pushed pretty hard, but they couldn't place me at the scene because I didn't even know where he lived, and we hadn't dated long beside that. They didn't let up, though, because they had no leads at all. In the middle of all that, Mom had her stroke and I came home. Those two detectives called a couple of times after I came home, but…they were mostly decent."

He nodded.

"Then, just recently an ER doctor who'd treated Mom when she was first taken to the hospital asked me out. I knew I shouldn't say yes. I *knew* it." She was probably crushing Tom's hand. "But I was still deluding myself. I kept telling myself the attack on Elliott didn't have anything to do with me. How *could* it?"

Emotions, or maybe thoughts, flickered over Tom's face. "Anything else going on back when this Elliott was attacked?"

"Yes, but I was big in denial about that, too. It was one of those weeks when I felt like a spider was crawling up the back of my neck. I kept whirling around, but there was never anyone there." Then she told him the rest of the weird stuff.

"I'm sure it goes without saying that the detectives there weren't interested in any of that."

"And here in Storm Lake? Have you noticed anything like that?"

"I get the creepy-crawlies sometimes, but people are always staring at me. Steve's death was like the biggest tragedy and scandal in Storm Lake history. There was plenty of controversy—he'd had so many friends, or really fans—that everyone thought they knew him. Football star, champion baseball pitcher? Prom king, knocking a woman around? Steve Dunn? Everyone thought I had to be lying. So I've been slinking around avoiding people I knew in high school or while I was married." And doing her best to avoid looking anyone in the eyes. "And remember, for the first month or two, I pretty much lived at the hospital. I ate three-quarters of my meals in the cafeteria. I wasn't on public display until Mom improved enough to come home and I actually started heading out on a regular basis to the grocery store, the pharmacy, the plant nursery, and working in plain sight in Mom's garden."

"I take it that brings us to the murder of the doctor. Colin Parnell?"

"Yeah. We had coffee, then a week later, dinner. He was killed that night after he got home."

Tom's gaze sharpened in a way that made her uneasy. "Someone was waiting for him?"

"They don't know, except whoever it was got into his house somehow. After arriving home—they also haven't figured out whether he went straight home or not—he apparently had time to make himself comfortable. He got a cup of coffee and was on his laptop in his home office. So it could have been half an hour after he got home, or two hours." She frowned. "Maybe the medical examiner nailed down the time closer than that. Like they'd tell me. All *I* know is that, bang, I'm the central suspect. One of the two cops who showed up the first time was a teammate and buddy of Steve's. He made his feelings about me crystal clear."

"I hope you pointed out that he was seriously biased."

"I did." She grimaced. "Not that Deputy Chief Bowen is much of an improvement. No, he is. He isn't rude, at least. I was going to lawyer up, but I haven't. What's the point? I didn't do it. I had no idea where Colin lived. I didn't know him that well. Except…he was funny and *nice*. He didn't deserve that. No one does. I can't keep my head in the sand anymore. I have to accept that he died because of *me*. Pete, I don't know. And thank God Elliott survived. But of all people to be killed, Colin was a compassionate doctor who followed how Mom was doing long after he was responsible for her. Why him?" She shook her head. "I have to believe now it was because I went out with him. He barely pecked me on the lips when he walked me to the door that night. There was no big romantic or passionate scene to make someone mad. It just doesn't make any sense!"

No, IT DIDN'T. Seeing her emotional fragility, Tom wanted to tug Jordan across the cushion that separated them and wrap her in his arms. Instead, he had to keep that distance. She'd expect him to maintain some doubt and might even be suspicious if he announced he was completely on her side and ready to fight the world for her. He had to hold back for his own sake, too. Because he had a job to do.

He had to *prove* this woman hadn't attacked any of those men. And that wasn't easy to do, mainly because they hadn't found the forensic evidence they needed either to clear her or point to other suspects. That was unusual in and of itself.

These attacks had to be meticulously planned after Jordan showed interest in a man. They were damned cold-blooded, and also clean. The killer knew how to avoid shedding trace evidence—although thanks to the plethora of cop shows and thrillers out there, everybody had some idea what not to do. Still, Tom didn't like the idea that one of Steve's best buddies was a cop who'd have learned on the job everything he needed to know to accomplish the perfect murder.

"Back to Elliott—?"

"Keefe."

"He doesn't remember whether his assailant appeared as soon as he walked in the door?" Shouldn't have used the word *assailant*, he thought, but she didn't seem to notice.

"No. He remembers parking in the garage, then going into the kitchen. After that, nothing. The head injury was bad enough, it could have wiped out hours from his memory. He wasn't discovered until the next day when he didn't come into work for some appointments." Jordan's forehead creased. "Why do you ask?"

"Just struck me you'd have had to drive like a bat out of hell to beat him home and be waiting for him."

"If only a neighbor had *seen* something. Maybe Colin would have survived, too, if he'd been found right away."

Given what Tom had seen in the autopsy report, there'd been no possibility of that. He only made a sympathetic sound.

He asked more questions, delving into the creep campaign, as she described it.

Her mouth twisted. "As things turned out, you don't know how much I wish I'd called the police. But…can you imagine what kind of response I'd have gotten? An anniversary card that you take as subtly threatening given the date you received it? Mightn't you have an admirer sending the bouquets, ma'am? Or could someone be expressing sympathy? One of your own knives left out on your counter? How can you be positive you weren't thinking about something else and took it out for some reason, then got distracted?" She made a soft, pained sound. "Even if I'd kept those notes, what are the odds they'd have any fingerprints on them except for the mail carrier's and mine? From the attitude I'm getting from police officers, they'd be sure I sent them to myself so I'd look innocent." She disentangled her hand from his and sat up, putting both feet on the floor. "The police want to blame me. They might as well be wearing blinders. Plainly, I can't trust that they'll really investigate without bias. In fact, I can't trust anyone wearing a badge. No matter what happens, I may never be able to again."

She might as well have punched him. It was all he could

do not to reel at the blow. She didn't know she'd taken aim against him, but she'd hit her target all the same. Tom couldn't even blame her. He had the impression from his couple of conversations with the detectives in Walla Walla that they really were looking for other possibilities. Chief Guthrie wasn't. He'd hired Tom to go undercover because he was so damn sure she was a killer. Tom wished he'd understood sooner how biased the police chief was. He might not have taken the job, or at least not agreed to go undercover.

Now…he wouldn't go back for a redo. Jordan too badly needed someone on her side—or at least impartial.

He turned his thoughts back to the latest event. Whoever had painted that word on Jordan's house and car last night was getting impatient. But was that because he believed passionately that she was guilty? Or was the killer trying to influence the local police department because she deserved to be punished for what he saw as a crime she'd gotten away with?

The obvious was the death of her husband. But even with family, it was hard to imagine anyone fixated enough on his or her grievance to be willing to murder several people in hopes of sending Jordan to prison. Steve Dunn had died almost nine years ago. Long time to hold on to this level of rage.

Tom still believed that was exactly what was happening, but had to circle back to the hard reality that nailing down her innocence to everyone's satisfaction wouldn't be easy. It was one of those conundrums: proving someone had done something was a snap compared to proving they *didn't*. That was the very reason the US justice system insisted on the concept of without a doubt.

If he succeeded, he could be Jordan's hero—until he confessed to lying to her from the beginning.

She was withdrawing before his eyes. In fact, she rose to her feet and said, "You've wasted a lot of time on us. I appreciate it, but I won't keep you anymore."

His stomach coiled. *"Wasted?"*

"Thank you for being here again today, but I think you should go home. You do have a life."

No, actually he didn't. As things stood, *she* was his life, but he could hardly say that. What he did say was, "Don't hesitate to call," and left because that's what she wanted.

IF MOM'S ROOTS weren't thirty years deep in this town Jordan positively hated at the moment, she would have seriously considered packing Mom up and moving with her. Selling the house, finding a community where not a soul knew them.

Peering through the blinds at a car that slowed down in front of the house before abruptly speeding up, she thought, *Uh-huh.* Because starting over had gone so well for Jordan before. If someone hated her enough to kill men he didn't even know, probably hadn't met, he could find her anywhere.

Anyway, she had a number of blessings to count. Number one on her list would be Mom's many friends who kept rallying around, whatever they thought about Jordan. The hospital and care workers had been amazing, too.

Tom Moore was on that list as well. Higher than he probably should be given what a short time she'd known him—and how much about him she didn't know—but from the night Mom took that fall, he hadn't failed her. How could that not scare her?

Thank heavens, the next morning she saw him back out

of his driveway and his big SUV disappear. Jordan wasn't sure how much longer she could have waited.

She told her mother what she was up to—minus her actual motivation—then assembled what she needed to detail the interior of her old car, unlocked all the doors and the trunk, and set to work. She searched the trunk first, in case another little surprise had been left for her, then vacuumed the thin carpet that covered the wheel well.

Classic avoidance: she started with the back seat, ashamed of the trash she'd ignored, then took out the floor mats, and vacuumed thoroughly.

Front seat, passenger side next. Ditto. More vacuuming, and she used a spray bottle and clean cloth to clean the door and dashboard.

She'd just wiped the glove compartment when she thought, *can't skip that*. Fortunately, there wasn't a lot in it except for the official papers, a flashlight and a few receipts.

By this time, her heart was hammering. Around to the driver's side. What if the license was *gone*? No, that would negate the whole purpose.

She took out the floor mats, shook them and vacuumed them, then groped under this seat, too. The first thing her hand touched on was Colin Parnell's Idaho State driver's license. For an instant, she let herself look at his face. He was one of those rare people who looked good in a DMV photo. Along with his warm smile, a hint of humor showed in his eyes.

Jordan shuddered and whisked it into her jeans pocket.

Just to be thorough, she kept searching. There was less trash here; she supposed she too often tossed receipts, paper napkins, whatever, on the passenger seat. But then she touched something stiff that might have kept the seat from sliding on its track if she ever had reason to move it.

She knew, even before she pulled it out. Another driver's license, this one from Washington State. Elliott looked straight at her from the photo.

Chapter Ten

Had this license been left on the seat, too, right after Elliott was attacked, but she'd hopped in with her arms laden and unknowingly brushed it off? Thank God there hadn't been any evidence that would have allowed those detectives to get a warrant. Why hadn't anyone ever said that each man's driver's license was missing? Maybe Elliott hadn't noticed until way later and hadn't associated it with the assault, but *someone* should have seen that Colin's was missing from his wallet.

She pushed this license into her other pocket, hurriedly finished her cleaning job, and dashed inside.

Who would believe her if she admitted finding these? But she shook her head instantly. Nobody.

The next question was, where best to hide them?

Because it had momentarily crossed her mind that Tom was the one person she might be able to talk to, she set about avoiding him. She waited until she saw him leave in his huge SUV before she set out to run, and once she pretended not to hear the doorbell when she knew it was him standing on the welcome mat. It wasn't right to keep depending on him when there was so much wrong with her life. Face it: she'd become a Jonah. Bad luck followed her. No, be honest: *deadly* luck followed her.

A few days after the vandalism, a photo of Mom's garage made the Storm Lake weekly newspaper. Thank goodness Jordan had carried the paper into the house along with that day's mail before she opened it to see the front page. In black and white, the words didn't have quite the same impact, but it was bad enough. The caption read, *Vigilantism in our town?*

At least it didn't say, *A killer in our town?*

The editor wouldn't have dared. That would have been inviting a lawsuit.

The article was brief, every word carefully chosen. The writer did remind any reader who'd forgotten that Jordan Hendrick, a graduate of Storm Lake High School, had killed her husband in self-defense eight and a half years ago. They didn't say, in *possible* self-defense, but the reminder alone whispered, *A killer does live in that house.*

Jordan slumped in her chair, aware of the murmur of voices from the kitchen where a speech therapist worked with Mom, but focused on her own whirling thoughts. There was no hope of hiding the paper from her mother. Poring over every page including the classifieds was part of her routine. She'd demand Jordan go buy another copy if this week's had apparently failed to be delivered. Anyway, someone would have a big mouth.

Not like Mom hadn't shuffled out onto the porch to see "KILLER" painted on her front window anyway.

Feeling sick, Jordan bent forward and rested her forehead on the table. Would this ever end?

The doorbell pealed, and she jerked. Maybe she'd be lucky and this would be a neighbor instead of cops back for round six or eight. She'd lost track.

It was Tom on the doorstep, and he looked mad. "Did you see your newspaper?"

She smiled wryly. "How could I miss it?"

"I'm sorry," he said simply, and stunned her by pulling her into his arms.

For a moment, she stood there stiffly…but then she collapsed against him. Not to cry, just because she *needed* his strength and solid body. She flung her arms around his waist and held on for dear life. That had to be his cheek resting on her head. His chest rumbled with words she didn't even try to make out. This felt like more than reassurance.

Jordan kept clinging even as awareness of him as a man, not a friend, stirred in her. His powerful thighs pressed hers, and her breasts were flattened on his broad, muscular chest.

She couldn't let him see what she was feeling. She didn't dare *feel* any of this. But when she finally summoned the will to step away, that involved lifting her head and looking at him.

His gaze flickered down to her mouth, and she knew: he was thinking about kissing her.

And right this second, there was nothing in the world she wanted more than that.

TOM DIPPED HIS HEAD, as he'd wanted to do almost from the first moment he set eyes on Jordan. He wouldn't have been surprised if she'd yanked away, or at least pretended she didn't know what was about to happen, but instead she parted her lips and—damn, was she rising slightly on tiptoe? Yes!

Her lips were soft and sweet, the hum in her throat exciting him. He pressed and nibbled, and waited while she did the same back. And then, God help him, he slid his tongue into her mouth, rubbing sensuously against hers. He didn't sense any resistance, but she met the kiss awkwardly, as if she didn't quite know what she was doing. Had it really been so long—?

She had to know how aroused he was. His hands had been moving without conscious thought on his part. One cupped her butt and lifted her. The other had slid up to her nape. He plunged his fingers in hair as silky as he'd imagined and held the back of her head so he could improve the angle for deep, long kisses that grew in urgency.

Jordan whimpered, and he thought he might have groaned. He needed to think this through…but right now, he wasn't capable of that kind of reason.

He ground his erection against her softer body and nipped her lip. She tried to climb him. Fine by him. He could help with that—

Background voices seemed to be gaining in volume.

"You're doing so well, Mrs. Hendrick! I don't think you're going to need me for much longer."

Tom tried to process that. He knew who *he* needed, but that didn't make sense. Then, suddenly, it did. Oh, hell! He and Jordan weren't alone.

He lifted his head, made himself lift Jordan away. "Sweetheart. Your mother is coming."

Her lashes fluttered. "What?" Then an expression of horror crossed her face and she backed into the doorframe with a bump. "Oh, no! What are we *doing*?"

Stung, he said, "We kissed. That's all."

"We can't let anybody *see* us," she cried…and his brain kicked back in gear.

She was right—and not only was the therapist coming, but also judging from the tap of the cane so was her mother. Worse yet, he and Jordan still stood on the threshold. Front door wide open, *any*one could have seen them.

"No, no!" Jordan keep retreating, expression panicked,

cheeks flushed…her eyes holding both shock and the remnants of passion. He hadn't been alone in that firestorm.

"Oh, Jordan," her mother called. "Is somebody here?"

Tom said, "Just me, Mrs. Hendrick. Wanted to check on you two." Remembering suddenly what he had come over for, he looked down, disconcerted, to see that he'd dropped the damn newspaper. In fact, he'd crumpled it beneath the sole of his boot.

"Did anybody drive by?" Jordan whispered urgently. "Or…or…"

Walk by? How would he know? He'd been that unconscious of their surroundings, something that hadn't happened to him in years. Cops couldn't *let* themselves be oblivious.

A lump in his throat, he said, "I don't know. But I'm taller and wider than you are. I doubt anyone could see past me."

"It wouldn't have been hard to tell what you were doing. And you wouldn't have been—"

Kissing her mother? Yeah, no stretch for an observer to guess his partner in that steamy embrace.

In a low voice, he said, "I'm not as vulnerable as the men who'd been attacked. You know I carry a gun." Would it make a difference if he'd introduced himself as a cop from the beginning?

Sure it would have—she wouldn't have given him the time of day.

After one wild look at him, she stepped to the side, giving a less than convincing smile to the middle-aged woman waiting for them to quit blocking the doorway. "Nora, thanks for coming."

Nora beamed, said goodbye to her patient, and trotted down the porch steps and to her car in the driveway as if she hadn't noticed anything.

Jordan's mother had been behind her, and probably hadn't, either. No, she was fussing because he was trampling on the newspaper, crumpling pages.

"This is my paper," he assured her mother. "I guess I dropped it."

Jordan took a deep breath. "Mom. There's a photo of the house on the front page. You know, with the spray-painting on it. That's why Tom came over. He wanted to be sure I'd seen it."

Mrs. Hendrick stared at them in bewilderment. "Why would they put something awful like that in the paper?"

Tom glanced at Jordan, who seemed speechless, and said gently, "I guess they think it's news. There was quite a fuss here, you know. I can't remember the last time I've seen so many official vehicles in one place."

Actually, in his world, that kind of gathering was common, but usually provoked by a shooting with fatalities. He could only imagine what the scene had looked like after he and Max had been gunned down. Funny, he'd never thought to ask who had called it in. As if it mattered...except that if there had been any greater delay, he probably wouldn't have survived.

"Why don't you sit down, Mom? Our copy of the paper is on the table."

Jordan wasn't meeting his gaze, or, really, looking at him at all. Shyness? Or something else?

"Tom," she added, "thanks for telling us. It's too late for us to do anything about it, but everyone in town is already talking about me anyway." Resignation dulled her voice. She was trapped and enduring. Her only way out would be to abandon her mother, and his gut said she'd never do that. That absolute loyalty tapped something vulnerable deep in him. He'd had friends, but never anyone he knew with complete certainty would never abandon him.

He had to clear his throat. "Give me a call if you want to take a run in the morning," he said, backed the rest of the way onto the porch, gathered up the torn pages of his newspaper and left.

As he ambled across the street, pretending nothing was out of the ordinary, he scanned sidewalks, lawns, the depths of front porches. If any of the neighbors were out front, he didn't see them. That didn't mean some hadn't seen the show, then scuttled out of sight to call everyone they knew.

There wasn't a lot of traffic on this street, especially at this time of day, but casual passersby weren't what worried him. What he had to wonder was how much time her stalker was able to give to spying on her, and where he hid. At this moment, utterly exposed, Tom knew exactly what Jordan meant when she described this feeling: as if a spider was crawling up his neck.

Even more disturbing was his realization that he couldn't have staged that kiss any better if he had plotted it. Chief Guthrie would be slapping him on the back in congratulations.

After the last guy she'd dated had been murdered so recently, Tom doubted she would be willing to be seen in public with any man, even if she felt something strong for him. In fact, the more she liked him, the *less* likely she'd be to agree to a date.

Unless, of course, she was the killer. Little though he believed that, his job required him to add the usual addendum.

Either way, Tom had just accomplished much the same purpose as a date at whatever restaurant in town was most popular...assuming that embrace had been witnessed by the right—or wrong—person. Or that gossip reached that person.

There was a certain relief at letting himself into his rental house and locking the door behind him, even though somebody could be in the house already, waiting. That was improbable, but still he stooped and pulled his backup weapon. He listened to the silence before clearing the house, room by room.

He did feel just a little paranoid now. He'd already been sleeping with his gun close at hand, but he thought it might be smart to take other precautions.

Speaking of traps, he hadn't set this one…but he was very willing to take advantage of it.

TOM WAS ABOUT to set out to spend a couple of hours in his fake office before picking up groceries when his phone rang. Jordan.

"Hey," he said, going for relaxed, "you up for a run?"

He hadn't seen her leave that morning, but he'd sure as hell seen her coming back, tearing down the street as if a pack of vicious wolves was snapping at her heels.

There was a short silence. Then, "I've already been. It was weird. I thought… Oh, never mind." She drew a shuddery breath. "I'm seeing shadows, that's all."

"Why didn't you ask me to run with you?" he asked gently.

"You know why. I can't be seen with you."

He felt a wrench in the vicinity of his heart. He didn't mind being needed; he'd protect her in any way he could. He wished he believed she trusted him—even though she shouldn't.

"I'd rather you did ask me," he assured her, marveling at his calm voice.

Damn, this had him as dizzy as if he were staggering off the kind of carnival ride that was fun when you were a kid but that he wouldn't be caught dead on anymore. Up, down, all around.

He cared about Jordan Hendrick more than he wanted to admit, even—maybe especially—to himself. He could fall for her. But always, the cynical side of him that he'd learned as an unwanted kid and honed as a cop murmured, *There's no way to prove she was followed. Did she just want to throw that out there?*

"This one of those times you felt that spider crawling up your back?"

"Something like that." She chuckled, although he didn't buy it, said, "Maybe we can run Wednesday," and pretended she needed to help her mother with something unnamed.

Tom closed his eyes. He shouldn't have agreed to this. Originally, it had seemed straightforward, as undercover work went. Keep an eye on the woman living across the street from him. Befriend her if he could. Prevent anyone from attacking her even as he tried to trick her into going after *him*.

Don't feel too much.

And lucky him, his plan for the day was to spend a couple of hours in his fake office, then break for lunch with Chief Guthrie, who insisted again on a face-to-face. Fortunately, one woman without much of a social network was unlikely to hear that he was hanging out with the police chief.

JORDAN WOULD HAVE been happier not to leave the house again today, but Mom started fretting about one of her medications due for a refill.

"I forgot to ask you to call it in yesterday. I'm sorry."

"It's fine. Are you completely out?"

"No, not until tomorrow, but…" Mom would worry until she had a nice, full bottle safely tucked in her medicine cabinet.

"I'll call and then go pick it up." Jordan smiled. "Won't hurt me at all." She could go while the caregiver who helped Mom bathe was here.

An hour later, she went out to her car. She didn't see any hint of movement up or down the street. Tom's big vehicle wasn't in his driveway. She should quit noticing if it was there or not, except…she couldn't help feeling reassured when she knew he was close and would come running if she called.

The pharmacy was downtown, and she had to park a block away. Once inside, she fidgeted as she waited in line while pharmacy techs searched, seemingly in slow motion, for the prescriptions people ahead of her had come in for.

Once her turn had come and she'd paid, she glanced at her watch and realized that hadn't taken as long as she'd thought. Being on edge all the time—swiveling her head constantly to see who came in the door, who was in each aisle—seemed to stretch the minutes torturously.

Maybe she'd treat herself to a latte. Betty's Café had served nothing but plain coffee when Jordan lived here before, but was apparently doing a booming business once an espresso bar was added.

She could treat herself, even if the caffeine wasn't ideal given her state of mind. But, heck, she wouldn't get the jitters until she was safely home again.

The booths and tables were mostly occupied, she saw at a glance, not surprising at around one o'clock. She walked briskly past several tables to the bar, careful not to look at anyone.

She'd given her order and was waiting when a deep but

low voice coming from a nearby booth penetrated. Was that Tom? Why wouldn't it be? By this time, he must have made other friends.

Unable to resist looking, she saw only the back of his head. But across the table from him...that was Storm Lake Police Chief Guthrie. Uniform, badge and all. An empty plate pushed away, he appeared intent on his conversation with Tom.

For some reason, her heart thudded in a heavy beat. They might know each other because Tom was responsible for law enforcement in the county parks. They might—

"I think I've set myself up." Tom's voice filled a lull in the overall chatter. "She'll never be willing to go out with me—she's afraid even to run with me in case we're seen together too often, but we did have a...moment on her front porch. If anyone was watching..."

The chief leaned forward. "A moment."

Frozen, she waited. Tom wouldn't say. He wouldn't—

"A kiss."

She didn't analyze what she heard in his voice. It didn't matter.

"This is our chance," he said.

Behind her, the barista called, "Jordan!"

As if everything around her had gone into slow motion, Jordan saw Chief Guthrie's gaze pass Tom to lock on her. Tom turned to look over his shoulder and met her eyes. His expression was appalled.

Jordan backed away. One step, another. She bumped into a diner seated at a table, then whirled and ran.

Chapter Eleven

"Well, damn. There's a good plan down the tubes." Guthrie sounded annoyed.

Every muscle locked into battle mode, Tom just looked at him. He'd never in his life wanted more to say *I told you so*, but he did currently work for this man.

Sliding out of the booth, he stood, said, "I'll see what I can do to patch things up," took the tall cup labeled with Jordan's name from the barista and walked out.

Yeah, who was he kidding? Everyone knew that no glue ever made could patch trust, once broken.

Convince her we're on her side. Spying on her to protect her.

Stomach roiling, Tom wished he hadn't eaten that burger and greasy fries.

He drove home on autopilot. He'd try to talk to her, but then what? Start wearing his badge and gun openly, maybe walk into the police station and introduce himself as the new lieutenant heading investigations? Or would Jordan let him continue passing under the radar as far as the rest of the world was concerned?

Talk to her first.

Turning the corner, he saw her car in the driveway. He parked in his own, sat unmoving for too long, then grabbed her drink and got out. Somehow, he knew she'd hear the slam of his door. His knock wouldn't be a surprise.

That she answered the knock *was* a surprise. Her face was cold and set as she stepped out on the porch and shut the door behind her.

"Your mother is napping?"

She didn't bother responding to that. She did take the cup from his hand and set it on the broad railing. Then she crossed her arms.

"This is the last time I'll open that door for you or speak to you. I'll ask you not to try to bypass me and go to my mother for any reason whatsoever." Pure ice.

"Jordan, will you listen? Give me a chance to explain?"

"That you were hired to wriggle your way into my life and find evidence that I'm the killer the police want me to be?" She made a harsh sound. "Given their tunnel vision, I should have suspected. Are you a PI or a cop yourself?"

Voice rough, he said, "Cop. I'm a detective."

"Of course you are. Well, you can tell Chief Guthrie that I'm through speaking to you or his detectives without an attorney being present. I was a fool."

The flash of pain in her eyes had him stepping forward. "Will you listen?"

She studied him with contempt. "You've lied to me from the beginning. Every word. Why would I believe anything you say? Isn't what you're saying now a lie, too? Just a new, expedient story." She shook her head. "Please leave, and don't step foot on this property again. Do you hear me?"

"I can help you. Keep you safe." Damn, was he begging? "I don't believe you ever hurt anyone."

"But I did, didn't I?" The one sentence was both scathing and filled with pain.

"I mean it," he said to her back.

She grabbed her to-go cup and opened the door.

Before she could shut him out once and for all, he said, "Don't tell anyone I'm a cop."

Jordan went still.

"Help me keep my cover so I can catch the scum who murdered the doctor."

She hesitated before giving an abrupt nod and disappearing inside. Tom heard the dead bolt slide shut with steely finality.

FORTUNATELY, MOM APPARENTLY hadn't heard the knock.

When she appeared after her nap, she used a cane instead of the walker, demonstrating her increased steadiness. She must have brushed her hair on the way, too.

Jordan was struck again by how much she'd improved. In the absence of another feared stroke, Mom might not truly need her for that much longer.

Dishing up leftover potato salad, she wondered if it was too late to apply to the University of Idaho or other schools for fall semester to finish her BA. If she stayed in Idaho, she could claim in-state tuition and be close to her mother, too. She wanted so much to believe she had a future.

Except, moving on was a fantasy until the killer trying to set *her* up was arrested, tried and convicted.

I can help you. Help me keep my cover so I can catch the scum who murdered the doctor.

Could he? Would he?

Anger seared her. *Sure. You betcha. Mr.—no, Detective Trustworthy.*

The one who'd kissed her as if he meant it, then bragged about it to his boss because really, he'd positioned her where anybody might see and done it because a date wasn't happening, and he was getting desperate. Not desperate for *her*, but for a triumphant closure for his case.

Thank God she hadn't told him about those driver's licenses.

Her eyes and even sinuses burned, but if tears were responsible, she wasn't about to let them fall. She joined her mother at the table and helped herself to servings of potato and fruit salads she didn't want.

For the second time in her life, she'd let herself fall for a man. Jordan had to marvel at her own judgment. *Fool me once*, she thought, but she hadn't learned anything. Look how spectacularly she'd been fooled the second time.

Never again.

She went through the motions of a normal afternoon and evening. She vacuumed, scrubbed the downstairs bathroom, made and pretended to eat dinner, watched a streaming show Mom liked without hearing a word herself, showered, and helped Mom with bedtime tasks. This was why she'd come home. For now, she was needed, and always loved as long as her mother lived.

But no matter what she did, no matter how firm her vow, her thoughts spun.

How could Tom Moore live with himself? Or was that even his real name? He'd pretended ignorance about her, then listened to her story with compassion and intelligence. Fake compassion, probably real intelligence. Too late, it was easy to imagine Tom weighing her every word, slotting pieces into place and seeing the gaps. His kindness the night her mother fell. Was that real, or had he been on the clock the entire time, gloating at the chance to build trust with her?

Was he a runner at all? Had everything he'd told her about the parks been gleaned from the city and county websites and maybe a few career articles: So You Want to Be a Park Ranger. San Francisco? For all she knew, he'd visited the city once or twice.

Of everything he'd said, Jordan was most inclined to believe he'd been shot. His stiffness and grimaces of pain looked too genuine. She'd bet cops were shot a whole lot more often than park rangers.

His strength when he held her, his tact and kindness with Mom, those hurt to remember. The part she'd never forgive him for was the heat in his eyes when he looked at her. Either he had somehow faked it, which she doubted given his erection—or he'd have been happy to take her to bed because, hey, she was a woman, he was bored, why not? She'd be mad at him when she found out the truth anyway, so what was one more betrayal?

Jordan pulled down the covers and sat on the edge of her bed, exhausted but knowing what would happen when she lay down and closed her eyes. She'd keep picturing Tom's every expression, the way amusement crinkled the skin beside his eyes, the deeper groove in his left cheek when he laughed or gave her a wickedly sexy grin. His impatience with the unruly waves in his hair, his funny stories, the warm clasp of his hand.

Him.

Two nights later, she was still going through the motions. Sleep remained elusive, her dreams disturbing. About to get into bed, she heard her mother call, "Jordan?"

She found Mom dumping out the contents of the drawer from her bedside stand on her bed.

"Mom? What are you doing?"

"You know I have asthma. I suddenly couldn't remember—"

Oh God—was she struggling for breath? She was definitely breathing hard.

"Isn't it usually brought on by allergies, or when you get a cold?"

"Yes, but—I'm going to have an attack! I know I am, and I can't find my inhaler."

Jordan felt almost certain that her mother was getting worked up only because she'd suddenly thought about the asthma that hadn't once reared its head since Jordan came home, and then got to thinking about where she left her inhaler.

Almost was the key word. What if…?

Jordan joined the hunt, finding and searching her mother's purse, the bathroom, the kitchen junk drawer, between cushions anywhere Mom might have sat in the living room. Under the bed. She delved into the pockets of her mother's coats and bathrobe, checked an old purse. By the time she had to concede defeat, Mom was panting for breath.

"I'll call your doctor."

"It's the middle of the night!"

"He's part of a clinic. I bet they have someone on call. If not, we'll go to the ER."

There was indeed a doctor on call, who agreed to phone in a prescription to the hospital pharmacy. Jordan just had to go get it.

Her mother had calmed, and Jordan became even surer that this was all unnecessary, but it was also true that Mom had lost control of so much of her life. She'd definitely become fixated on her medications, as if they were the armor that kept her from disaster. Who could blame her?

"I'll call Jennifer Pierce," Jordan decided. The Pierces lived three houses down. Jennifer wasn't as close to Mom as several other neighbors, but she was considerably younger.

Getting up in the middle of the night and making it over here wouldn't be as big a deal for her as it would for Mrs. Chung, for example. "I won't be gone long."

Jennifer's husband answered the phone, and Jennifer immediately agreed to come over. He came with her and said he'd stay, too. Of course he did. After all, this was the house where an accused killer lived.

Jordan thanked them and said, "I think she's okay now, but if breathing really becomes difficult, call 911."

While waiting, she'd already scrambled into her clothes, and she hustled out now. Something moved in the darkness between the house and garage, so she threw herself into her car and locked the doors. As she stared in a vain attempt to see a person or dog or cat that might have jumped onto a garbage can, she turned on the car to warm it up.

Shivering, she knew she'd been imagining things. She did that a lot these days. She was not being watched 24/7, no matter how it felt.

Annoyed at herself, she drove the all-too-familiar route to the hospital. Fifteen minutes, she'd be home, Mom could take a couple of puffs on the inhaler, and they'd all get some sleep.

RESTLESS, TOM TRIED to stay too busy to brood. He sat at the kitchen table working on his laptop. Maybe he *should* break cover. That would allow him to seriously investigate everyone close enough to Jordan's deceased husband to hold a grudge. Given that he hadn't been able to interview anyone, what information he'd gathered from databases had been more sparse than he liked.

The best he'd been able to do today was peruse the high school's yearbooks, which were online. He'd already seen DMV and news photos of Steve Dunn, but studied these of the guy who was, as Jordan had said, obviously a star in the eyes of his classmates. In the senior yearbook, he was in at least a dozen photographs aside from his class photo. Football and baseball teams, live action photos during games, being crowned homecoming king—no sign of Jordan there, Tom noted—even student council. Chosen most likely to become famous.

Really?

The kid was good-looking in an unfinished way, buff but probably not big enough for major colleges looking for linemen, and he had a grin that would have impressed Tom more if he didn't know what a piece of you-know-what he'd turned out to be.

Of course, Tom looked up Jordan in the several yearbooks. She was just as pretty as he thought she was now, but noticeably shy, or maybe just reserved. Didn't wear a lot of makeup, didn't look polished the way more confident girls did.

Tom searched out Steve's sister and brother, too. The sister, Carolyn, was a year older than Steve. She had some of the reserve, even watchfulness, that Jordan did, making Tom wonder what her home life had been like.

Kevin Dunn was two years younger than his brother and had some of the same shine but not quite at the same level. He played football, too, running back because he wasn't as big as his brother. Not as many photos in the yearbooks. No prom crowns. Question was, did he resent his big brother, or idolize him? Or both?

Tom wondered if other people would know. Man, he wanted to talk to the guy.

He noted the names of boys on the sports teams, underlining the ones who seemed especially buddy-buddy with

Steve in candid photos. Bussert—or Buzz, according to a caption—fell into that hanger-on category.

The list he made of girls who posed with Steve, or appeared to be part of his crowd, was shorter. Tom didn't see a single picture of the great and glorious Steve Dunn with the girl he'd married months after their high school graduation.

He started by searching for information on those people in the intervening decade plus. A few popped up with criminal records, including Kevin Dunn. He'd had a couple of DUIs and been tagged for bar fights, although he hadn't actually done time. So—a short temper, like his brother. He'd worked for four different roofing companies since he graduated from high school two years behind Steve and Jordan. Maybe moved around for a better salary or because of layoffs, maybe not. He'd married a couple of years after high school, and his wife had been active on Facebook but seemed to have gone quiet, without a post in the past eight months.

Sister Carolyn was married, waited tables at a restaurant Tom hadn't yet been in, and had two children, according to her Facebook page, which was only sporadically updated.

Buzz had a sealed juvenile record, which interested Tom a good deal given his speculation about the pristine crime scenes. He'd ask Guthrie about it.

Tom starred names that jumped out at him for one reason or another. Eventually, his eyes began to cross and a headache defied the painkillers he took. He still had some of the heavy-duty stuff, which he rarely used anymore because it knocked him on his butt. Right now, he particularly had to be on his guard. If the kiss had worked as bait...

He flinched, ashamed of himself. Okay, yeah, purely by accident that kiss had presented an opportunity in this investigation. But there were things a man kept his mouth shut about, and this was one of them. Jordan had plenty of reasons to be furious, even if she didn't care enough about him to be hurt—and he thought she had been.

Damn it, he'd *known* it would come to this, one way or another, but hadn't expected that he'd feel as if he lay bleeding on the ground again. How could he have failed so spectacularly in letting himself forget that nothing between them was real? That was especially ironic, considering how stunned he'd been by a kiss that felt so damn perfect. For a fleeting instant, he'd felt as if he had held everything he could ever want in his arms.

He was afraid he knew where that had come from.

You have been given a chance to have all that. He'd known exactly what Emilia was talking about: a wife, kids, happiness. With her words in the back of his mind, had he wanted to see something with Jordan that wasn't real? The unexpected byway his life had taken might be responsible for that hollow inside that wanted to be filled.

Or had he just blown the chance he'd never expected to have?

With a groan he closed his laptop, slid it into a sleeve and then in a cupboard with pans and lids where it wasn't obvious.

He turned off the light above the stove, reached for the switch for the overhead light but frowned at seeing the only other light he'd left on was in the bathroom. He'd cleared the house, but the window locks in particular were inadequate and the one on the back door less secure than he liked.

Note to self: even if this was a rental, add a dead bolt to the back door tomorrow.

Frowning, he flicked off the light and started down the short hall to the bedrooms and single bathroom. He wondered if he'd be able to sleep at all—or whether he dared.

The air behind him stirred. If he hadn't already been in a heightened state of awareness, he wouldn't have moved fast enough. As it was, he jumped sideways and a club—no, a metal bar—slammed into his shoulder instead of his head. He started to spin while falling into the open door to an unused bedroom.

Pop.

Shot fired!

Tom dived for the floor and pulled out his backup piece, rolling to face the dark doorway. He had to see his assailant. The dark shape gave him no answer.

"Drop it!" he yelled.

Pop, pop. Suppressor.

He pulled the trigger of his own weapon. Once, twice. Running footsteps told him he'd delayed too long.

He shoved himself to his knees, intent on pursuing when he heard the back door hitting the house, but his left arm hung uselessly at his side and he staggered into a wall once he reached his feet.

He couldn't decide if the iron bar had dealt the worst blow, or the bullet. Or, hell, had there been two?

Tom carefully lowered himself to his knees again, propping his good shoulder against the wall to keep himself from going all the way down, and pulled his phone from his pocket.

Chapter Twelve

Two blocks from home, Jordan saw flashing lights. Mom! Oh, no. Had she really had a major asthma attack, after Jordan hadn't believed her? Or had worse happened since Jordan called Jennifer from the hospital?

Terrified, she strained to see. There was a police car with flashing lights in her driveway, but the ambulance was in Tom's, another police unit at the curb in front of his rental. For an instant, she didn't understand, but then a cold trickle entered her veins.

He'd been assaulted, just like the men she'd dated. What if he was dead?

Given how he'd betrayed her, she didn't expect the anguish. She braked hard at the curb in front of her house. She'd barely jumped out and reached the sidewalk when a police officer planted himself in front of her, gun held with his arms outstretched, and yelled, "Freeze! Hands in the air! Drop whatever you're holding!"

The cold turned to ice. The small paper bag holding the inhaler fell to the concrete. Shaking, she said, "I live here. This...this is my house."

"Turn around!" he snapped.

Turning let her see Tom's house where medics were carrying an unmoving patient out to the ambulance. The anguish heightened, as did her fear.

"I don't understand." But, oh, she did. The police here had made up their minds about her long since. Her mind flickered back to what she'd thought was motion, and now she knew she'd been right. *Someone* had seen her leaving the house, oh, so conveniently.

The memory was wiped out when, next thing she knew, the cop had grabbed her left hand and wrenched it down. A metal cuff snapped closed on her wrist. She struggled instinctively as he forced her other hand down and cuffed it, too. He grabbed her by the scruff of her neck and shoved her forward. She stepped off the curb without seeing it and fell hard onto the street, trying to take her weight onto her shoulder but ending up with her face skidding on the gritty pavement. She was momentarily dazed.

"What's going on?" another voice called. This one she knew—Deputy Chief Bowen, who had a conscious or unconscious swagger to impress onlookers with his authority even when he didn't wear a uniform, like tonight. He'd probably been getting ready for bed, she realized, or even *in* bed when the call came.

"Ms. Hendrick just arrived home. Real convenient timing."

He loomed over her, staring down with typical contempt. "What's she doing on the ground?"

"Fell after I cuffed her."

"Okay. Hoist her up. We need to take her in."

"Why?" she cried. "What happened?" Her view of him was distorted, just a tall figure rearing over her.

"Oh, I think you know exactly what happened. Once you get her loaded, search her car," he ordered.

Scared as she was, anger sizzled, too. "Do you have a warrant?"

"I have probable cause." And oh, how smug he sounded.

"I can prove where I was. But I'm not saying another word until I'm given the opportunity to call an attorney to be with me. And if you search my car without a warrant, count on a lawsuit."

The silence didn't tell her whether she'd intimidated them in the slightest or whether they were only pausing to watch the ambulance back out of the driveway and accelerate in the same direction she'd come from.

Despite herself, she pictured Tom smiling at her, and prayed, *Don't die. Please don't let him be too badly hurt.*

Another of the SUVs the Storm Lake PD liked rolled up to the curb, the lights blinding her. Jordan turned her head away to rest her other cheek on the road surface. When she did, salty blood trickled into her mouth.

A door slammed. "You arrested Ms. Hendrick?" the police chief asked.

"Ah...not officially. Just made sure she couldn't go for a gun."

"Does she have one on her?"

"Doesn't look like it." The original officer sounded nervous. "I haven't patted her down."

"Well, help the woman up!" the chief growled. "Then do it."

They essentially had to pick her up and set her on her feet. She closed her eyes and held herself rigid as a strange woman officer's hands groped her.

"Nothing, sir. I was going to look in her car, but she said she'll sue if we do."

Chief Guthrie snorted, but said, "We'd best have a talk with her first. What's that on the sidewalk?"

"I don't know. I made her drop it."

One of the men walked over and picked up the small sack. Paper rustled. "Uh, I think it's an asthma inhaler."

"What?"

She refused to look at them, but from the sound of it they were passing the sack around and peering inside.

Mad as it made her to ask for anything, she finally said, "Would one of you please take that to the house? My mother was short of breath. It's for her."

That elicited some discussion, but after a minute, one of them moved away.

"Well, let's take Ms. Hendrick to the station—"

"No," she said.

"Don't think this is your decision," the chief remarked.

"I called a neighbor to sit with my mother. She and her husband can tell you when I left. The receipt in that bag will tell you when I paid for the inhaler at the hospital. I drove straight home. I didn't have time to do whatever you think I did." Should she have even said that much? "Now, I want to call an attorney."

"Plenty of time for that," Bowen declared. "You can use the phone once you're at the station."

Bowen and the officer she didn't recognize muscled her into the back of one of the vehicles. The chief had apparently walked away, maybe to talk to another officer across the street at Tom's house.

With her arms wrenched behind her, Jordan's shoulders ached, the pain sharper in the right one she'd fallen onto. Her head hurt, too. It must have bounced when she went down. No wonder her brain felt rattled.

She stared at the back of the officer's head while he drove her the ten minutes to the city police station. He wasn't any gentler pulling her out, even though she didn't fight him.

She was aware of some stares as she was hustled to a windowless room and propelled into a wooden chair. There she sat for what felt like an hour, but probably was more like fifteen minutes. It was Chief Guthrie and Deputy Chief Bowen who walked into the room then.

She turned to look at them, hoping her stare incinerated them.

"You have *no* evidence connecting me to these crimes. After the way I was treated tonight, I'm going to bankrupt this city. I swear I will. Now, uncuff me and give me a phone."

They remained solid instead of crumbling into the hot cinders of her fantasy. The muscles in Chief Guthrie's jaw did flex before he circled behind her. A moment later, her hands fell to her sides. She stifled the groan.

A phone and the skinny local phone directory appeared on the table in front of her.

"Leave me alone." They'd be able to listen from outside the room, she felt sure, but right now she wanted the illusion of privacy.

The selection of local attorneys was skimpy, but one name leaped out at her. Susan Throndsen was an ardent gardener and longtime friend of Jordan's mother. She also happened to be a criminal attorney who'd moved here, if Jordan remembered right, after her partner died, and she'd practiced for ten years or more in Portland, Oregon.

Given the time of night, she was surprised when a woman picked up on the third ring. Jordan fumbled an explanation.

"This is Susan Throndsen," she said. "I remember you, Jordan. Where are you?"

"At the police station."

"I have to throw on some clothes, but I'll be there in twenty minutes or so. Don't say another word to anyone until I get there."

Jordan struggled with a lump in her throat. "Thank you."

TOM WAS AWAKE through the ordeal in the ER, unlike last time. They sedated him while a surgeon dug out the bullet, but he felt clearheaded surprisingly fast. They must have used a local instead of full anesthesia.

Suddenly a doctor stood above him, surgical mask pulled down to reveal the face of a man in his forties, at a guess. "Mr. Moore, we've removed a bullet from your shoulder, and cleaned and bandaged a slice on your thigh that must have been a bullet graze. I believe you suffered a head injury, too, although any concussion doesn't appear serious. We'll be keeping you for the night, though." He hesitated. "Either you make a practice of living dangerously, or you were struck by a barrage of bullets at some point."

"Barrage," Tom managed to say through a dry mouth. Was still supposed to be undercover? Clearly no one had told the surgeon that he was a cop.

The surgeon's eyebrows climbed, but he said only, "You'll be doing some rehab for that shoulder. I doubt that's a surprise to you."

"No."

The man patted his good shoulder, said, "Glad it wasn't worse," and departed.

A nurse took his place a minute later and slipped some ice chips into Tom's mouth. He was moved from what looked like recovery to a curtained space in the ICU. He desperately wanted to talk to Guthrie, to know what happened after he went down, but the man didn't show up.

Tom would have given a lot to be able to say, convincingly, *It wasn't Jordan*, but unfortunately he couldn't. From what little he'd seen, his assailant was shorter than him, and could conceivably be a man or woman. Man, he thought, from the breadth of shoulders, but it had all happened so fast.

God, he hoped they hadn't jumped to the conclusion that

it was Jordan who'd attacked him and come down hard on her. Either way, she hadn't rushed to his side.

And why would she do that?

He let his eyelids sink closed and realized how much he wished she *was* here, firmly holding his hand. Her scent was distinctive enough he'd be comforted even when he couldn't keep his eyes open. Last time, his lieutenant had been the first person he saw after regaining consciousness, and Yates had assumed Tom didn't need anyone sitting at his side. Nothing in Tom's background explained why this time he ached for someone—not just someone, Jordan—to care enough to come right away and stay with him.

Instead, he saw her face when she understood that he had betrayed her.

SHE AND SUE sat in that claustrophobic room for some time while a police officer drove to Jordan's house to retrieve the receipt from her purchase at the hospital pharmacy. For all she knew, Jennifer had dropped it in the wastebasket, but at least she had been able to locate it.

Chief Guthrie sat across the table from Jordan and her attorney and said woodenly, "Mrs. Pierce had the time of your call on her phone, and took a guess at how long it took her and her husband to get dressed and get to your house. She said you talked for a couple of minutes about what to do if your mother had a crisis."

Jordan didn't speak. All she wanted was to go home, take a hot shower and crawl into bed, after reassuring her mother. The only positive she could think of right now was that, while Tom had been shot, the chief said his recovery was likely to be swift.

"Mrs. Pierce also mentioned that you called later to check on your mother, saying that you were sitting in the parking lot at the hospital." His eyes narrowed. "You could just as well have called while you were driving. That opens the possibility you had a few minutes more than the timing you're claiming, but I'll admit that gap isn't a large one."

"It's ludicrously small, and you know it!" the attorney snapped. "Have you yet interviewed Detective Moore?"

He clearly didn't like that Jordan had given away the true identity of the wounded man, but had no right to complain.

"Deputy Chief Bowen spoke to him briefly. He didn't see his assailant well enough to give a description."

"What was this assailant wearing?" Sue asked drily. "Did it bear any resemblance to what my client is wearing? Or is she supposed to have managed a quick change in that infinitesimal *gap*, too?"

Guthrie transferred his gaze briefly to Jordan, who wore a Seattle Seahawks sweatshirt over leggings. Her bright blue parka had been torn in several places when she slid on the pavement.

"Ah...it was dark."

Sue drilled him with her gaze. "I'm placing you on notice that I will be pursuing remedies for the treatment doled out to Ms. Hendrick for no defensible reason by your officers. She would have willingly answered questions and did not in any way resist, yet she was held at gunpoint, cuffed, manhandled and injured although no arrest was made. I will be taking her to the hospital on the way home for a shoulder X-ray and to get her face and hands cleaned up." She stood, an athletic woman who might be fifty. Her graying dark hair was disheveled enough to suggest she hadn't stopped to brush it on the way out the door. As she helped Jordan stand up, she said quietly, "I thought better of you, Allen."

Jordan shuffled out the door ahead of her attorney, wishing she'd taken the time earlier—an eon ago—to put on socks as well as the wool felt clogs she wore as slippers. Although being cold for a few minutes going out to the car, into the hospital and out again was nothing compared to everything else about this evening.

During the drive, wishing the car heater would hurry to warm up, Jordan said, "I threatened to sue them."

"Their treatment of you was abominable. I think we need to follow through on that threat just on principle."

Thinking about Dr. Parnell, Jordan winced at having to walk into the ER. Did people working here know her name, and that she was a suspect in his murder? But Sue stayed at her side, insisted on an X-ray even though the physician felt sure Jordan's shoulder had only been wrenched, and watched as her face, hands and, yes, ankle, were cleaned, bits of gravel picked out, ointment applied and then bandaged.

Jordan almost opened her mouth and asked about Tom, who must have come through the ER, but restrained herself. He didn't *deserve* for her to care about him or worry about his injuries. She couldn't imagine he'd welcome a visit from her anyway. For all he knew, she'd been the one to shoot him. Although you'd think the police would have spent more time wondering what gun she'd used, and what she had done with it. Couldn't they have done that gunpowder residue test she'd read about in mysteries? Too late now, she thought, looking down at her hands, swathed in what seemed like an unnecessary amount of gauze.

Once Sue started the car again, Jordan said, "I don't think the Storm Lake department has a clue how to investigate a murder. Or an attempted murder. Assuming Detective Moore has the experience they need, they were dumb enough to put him in a position where he couldn't do anything but cozy up to me."

"Will you tell me more about that?" the attorney asked.

Jordan hesitated, then did, but kept her account abbreviated. Guthrie hadn't mentioned that passionate kiss in front of Sue, and Jordan would just as soon keep that to herself. The humiliation dealt to her tonight was bad enough, but admitting she'd fallen that far for his act was another story.

Sue walked her in at home, waiting while she fervently thanked the Pierces, who had stuck with Mom despite what they must be thinking about Jordan, and saw them out.

At last, Sue left, too, and Jordan thankfully locked the door, checked every window and the back door, and finally peeked in Mom's room to find her mother sound asleep.

And, no, according to Jennifer Pierce, Mom hadn't needed the inhaler. None of this needed to happen, not tonight, anyway. Once she knew Jordan had left to pick one up, she'd calmed down.

She had heard the to-do outside, meaning Jordan had a lot to tiptoe around come morning, but right now…the shower sounded blissful.

DISCHARGED, TOM ENDURED the ride in a wheelchair out of the hospital, then got stiffly into the back of a taxi. One of only two in town, he'd heard. Lyft and the like hadn't made it to a town this size. Guthrie had sounded a little embarrassed during his call that morning when he suggested that Tom make his own way home so as not to undermine his cover.

"Assuming it stays intact," he added. "We'll reimburse you for the cost of a taxi if you don't have anyone else who can pick you up."

Big of him, Tom couldn't help thinking.

"I don't want it to stay intact," he said. "It's time I investigate the way I should have from the beginning." He ended the call, not letting the chief argue. He didn't think there was anything else the subterfuge could accomplish.

The taxi driver offered to help him into his house, but Tom declined and limped up to the front door. Guthrie had thought to grab Tom's car keys and wallet last night, so Tom was able to let himself in. His backup piece had been taken into evidence in case he'd succeeded in wounding his assailant and the bullet turned up. Hard to imagine anyone lying in wait for him now, after the night's drama, but he still moved as quietly and cautiously as he could through the house, peering behind doors, making sure he was alone. Then he took his Sig Sauer 9-mm from the gun safe. He'd keep it close for comfort.

Back in the living room, he separated the blinds enough to peer out. The facade of the Hendrick house told him nothing. Worry sat like an indigestible meal in his belly. Guthrie had admitted in this morning's conversation that they'd hauled Jordan in last night to interrogate her, but that they'd ended up having to release her for lack of evidence. He'd been reluctant to say more.

Something in the chief's voice made Tom wonder. Had Jordan answered the door in her pajamas, hair sleep-mussed, maybe a pillow crease on her cheek? If so, how had they justified taking her in? Had they searched the house for a weapon and failed to find one? How far had they gone in their determination to nail her?

Did she finally hire a lawyer?

He found himself hoping so. She'd been naive in believing she could continue to answer questions so that the police would eventually rule her out and pursue other possibilities. Tom wished he'd looked deeper before he took this job. Yes, the murders clearly had some connection to Jordan, but Guthrie had jumped right on her as the only possible suspect. Tom hadn't let himself question that the way he should have. The job was convenient for him, the timing good for him to do this undercover gig.

He just hadn't understood what he'd be doing to a woman who might be innocent…and terrified.

Or that he'd be pathetically grateful if she'd just walk across the street, knock on his door and say, "I'm still mad at you, but I hope you'll be okay." If she'd give even a hint that she felt for him a fraction of what he felt for her.

The blinds in the front windows of *her* house didn't even twitch. And, damn, he needed to lie down, where he'd cuddle up to his handgun and, he felt sure, dream about another stint of agonizing physical therapy.

Chapter Thirteen

The squeak of a grocery store cart right behind her was enough to tighten the muscles in the back of Jordan's neck. Ridiculous, when she'd almost become used to unexpectedly coming face-to-face with people she'd hoped never to set eyes on again. That's the price you paid for a homecoming.

Annoyed at herself for cowardice, she glanced over her shoulder fully expecting to see someone she'd never met in her life grabbing a box of macaroni and cheese off the shelf. But no such luck.

Steve's mother stared at her, eyes blazing with hatred. The knuckles of her hands gripping the handles of the cart showed white. She'd aged drastically.

"You!" she spat, faced flushed red.

Jordan held her head high. "Hello—" Not "Mom" as she'd called this woman so briefly. "Nancy," she settled on.

"How dare you come back to this town and strut around as if you belong! I was glad—*glad*—to see that picture in the paper and to know someone had the guts to remind everyone that you *are* a killer. You should be serving a term in the state penitentiary, not going on with your life when Steve is dead because of you!"

Rustles from behind gave Jordan a bad feeling they had an audience now. Although what difference did it make?

"I know you loved your son," she said, as gently as she could. "I did, too. I tried—"

Last time they'd met face-to-face, Steve's mother had blamed Jordan for the fact that he hadn't had a chance to go on to play college ball and ultimately end up in the NFL. In her version, Jordan had demanded he marry her and give all that up.

Jordan had no idea where the woman had come up with that fantasy version of her son's life.

Now, of course, she all but shouted, "You shot him!"

Jordan continued as if she hadn't heard. "I tried to keep loving him even when he hurt me. You had to know what an ugly temper Steve had. I always wondered if he got it from his father. Whether you had to cower when he was alive, hide your bruises, pretend everything was fine when you watched him raising his boys to be just like him."

The nearly gaunt face drained of color.

Guilt flayed Jordan. From things Steve had said, she was almost certain about what this woman had endured. But, no matter what, she'd loved her child. How could she let herself believe he was as bad or worse than her husband? Steve had been her golden boy and always would be in her memory.

Did I think I could puncture her illusions? Jordan wondered.

Face now bone-white and lips thinned to reveal the unhappy lines that had worsened since Jordan knew her, Nancy Dunn's eyes flicked to whoever was eavesdropping behind Jordan.

"You're the monster," she whispered, voice shaking. "You've fooled everyone. Even now you killed another man, a good, respected man. I don't know how you keep getting away with it, but sooner or later, they'll see through you, and you'll be cuffed and behind bars. For Steve's sake, I can't wait."

She wheeled her cart around and rushed away down the aisle.

Jordan gritted her teeth and turned to see who had been avidly listening.

Three other shoppers averted their eyes and grabbed, probably at random, for items on the shelves. One was a woman who looked familiar, probably from high school. The others Jordan didn't offhand recognize, but clearly they all knew who *she* was.

Heat seared her cheeks, and she wanted to abandon her own half-full cart and flee, but pride and practicality wouldn't let her. She and Mom were low on groceries, and she didn't want to have to do this all over again. Maybe next week she'd drive to the next town that had a decent size store instead of shopping here in town.

Ashamed that she'd let herself become embroiled in a scene, she moved fast, barely glancing at her list. She didn't see anyone else she knew except one of the checkers. She chose a checker she didn't recognize, paid and left the store. Just outside the doors, she paused and looked carefully around before she dared venture into the parking lot.

What a way to live.

"I've known Bussert since he was a kid," Chief Guthrie said. He already sounded cautious. Possibly offended, too. "What are you suggesting?"

Phone to his ear, Tom lay back on the workout bench that had been one of his few additions to the furnished rental. "I'm saying he may have been one of Steve Dunn's best friends in high school. When he and Wilson knocked on Ms. Hendrick's door after the doctor's shooting, Bussert didn't even try to hide his hostility for her. When I started looking into the backgrounds of Dunn's close friends, the fact that one of your police officers has a sealed juvenile file leaped right out at me. You must have known it would."

It was difficult to interpret a silence. Was the chief trying to figure out how to finesse his way out of answering the question?

But instead of a curt response, Guthrie sounded chagrined. "To tell you the truth, I'd forgotten he and Dunn were friends. Got into trouble together a few times," he admitted. "Nothing big—just pranks."

Uh-huh.

"Kid had a temper. No surprise, his family was a mess. There were half a dozen domestic violence calls to that address, but Cody's mother was never willing to speak out against her husband. Sad woman. Cody attacked his own father in defense of his mother. I suspect it was justified, but he spent some time in detention and then a group home. By the time he earned his AA degree, I believed he'd turned himself around, and nothing's ever happened to make me doubt that judgment."

"He pretty clearly harbors anger at Ms. Hendrick."

"You taking her word on that?"

"You made sure he didn't go back to talk to her again," Tom said mildly.

"You've got me there. Wilson suggested he sit this one out."

"Normally, I'd want to interview Officer Bussert," Tom said. "But as things stand, I'll step back and let you do it."

"You're seriously considering him for this?" the chief asked incredulously.

"You have to know he's a possible. I want to know if anyone else in the department had a close relationship to the Dunn family as well."

"What the hell?"

Another call was coming in, and Tom recognized the number.

"I need to take a call," he said. Without compunction, he cut off Guthrie and answered. "Lieutenant Moore."

A woman's voice said, "Lieutenant, this is Detective Dutton from Walla Walla. Thought I'd update you and find out if anything has happened on your end."

The detective and her partner knew Tom had been working undercover, hoping to attract the attention of this perpetrator. He told her about the assault, and his regret that he'd neither gotten a good look at his assailant, nor taken him down.

"You still suspect Ms. Hendrick?" she asked.

"I don't, but the chief does. Just between us, I think he's reluctant to believe anyone in town he might have known for years could be this obsessive."

"Ms. Hendrick is a local, too," Detective Dutton pointed out.

"But hasn't lived here in some years. When she did, she stayed in the background." She'd apparently excelled at that. "I doubt Chief Guthrie ever met her."

"Ah."

"You said you have an update?"

He'd be glad for any new tidbit he could chew on—or that might lead to the real killer.

"You know Ms. Hendrick caught our attention because a man she'd dated briefly was murdered only days after she'd last seen him."

"Pete Shroder." That was the guy who had seemingly

interrupted a burglar, or a team of them, in the act of cleaning out his house.

"Right. Well, a couple of days ago, a fingerprint we ran from the scene finally popped." She sounded quietly satisfied. "Belongs to a man named Bill Bannan." She spelled the last name. "He and a partner were just arrested in the act of carrying a fancy big-screen TV out of a house in Eugene, Oregon. Real nice house, apparently. They'd pretty well emptied it, and once local police had addresses, they found both the men's garages filled with stolen items. We're hoping they'll find something that came from Shroder's house, although after all these years, that would be a stroke of unexpected luck. Nonetheless, I think we can assume they—or at least Bannan—were responsible for Pete Shroder's death."

"So only the assault on Elliott Keefe can be linked to Jordan—Ms. Hendrick," he corrected himself.

"That's correct. We'd probably have done no more than interview her once if it hadn't been for Shroder's unsolved murder."

"Was her name mentioned publicly in connection with that investigation?" Tom asked.

"I'll have to check, but yes, a reporter from the *Walla Walla U-B* got her name somehow." She offered to email the article to him.

They parted on that promise, and his reciprocal one: he'd let her know when or if they got a big break here in Storm Lake.

Detective Dutton didn't dawdle. Within fifteen minutes, Tom had his laptop open and was reading the relevant article about what was apparently a rare, mysterious murder for the college town. And yes, there was the name, Jordan Hendrick.

He sat staring at it, highlighted in his imagination. What-ifs could be pure fantasy, but this time, he thought he was onto something.

What if the real killer had happened on this article, maybe because he'd hated Jordan all along and done regular Google searches for her name? What if the murder gave him an idea? The police had spoken to her because she'd so recently dated a man who was then murdered. What if it happened again? And maybe again? What if the police could be convinced to arrest her? She hadn't been held accountable for Steve Dunn's death, but wouldn't the next best thing be setting her up to serve a long, long sentence in prison for murdering another man?

If so, the idea obviously took a while to firm up. Might have initially been no more than a kind of revenge fantasy. Only then, because his rage grew for some reason, that fantasy became a real possibility to him.

As a scheme, it was diabolical and in some ways impractical…but Jordan had been a hairbreadth away from being arrested for Dr. Parnell's murder. If Tom had died—

She'd never been in his house. Her fingerprints wouldn't have been found. But sooner or later, this killer might come up with a way to be sure her fingerprints or even something that belonged to her *was* found at a crime scene. Or the other way around; suppose cops found something from one of the men's homes, as if she kept trophies. Planting an item wouldn't be difficult. He thought uneasily about her car, sitting unguarded in the driveway.

Then he thought, hell, had she handled anything *he'd* taken home? The newspaper that had fallen to their feet came to mind, but he was sure she hadn't touched that. Anyone could root in the garbage or recycling cans, though.

If it wasn't too late, Tom would have searched his own

house to be sure that hadn't already happened. He'd have heard by now if anything connected to Jordan had been found, though.

Thank God, he thought. Time to have a talk with Chief Guthrie. Turned out there was good reason for him to hide his real job here in Storm Lake after all.

He wanted some cooperation in checking the work schedules and vacation time of anyone in the department who'd had a connection with Dunn. Even while he was following that thread, assuming Guthrie didn't balk, they could goad the killer with a newspaper article that discussed the doctor's murder and the attempted murder of park ranger Tom Moore, but had no mention of Jordan's name at all. The police spokesperson—who might well be Guthrie himself—could imply that initial leads had fizzled and they were left with a real puzzler, but felt confident that sooner or later they'd solve the case. They could even hint that they were pursuing a new possibility.

Wouldn't *that* enrage someone trying to pin these crimes on Jordan?

The danger was that this would push this nutcase to give up on the idea of making Jordan's life hell by getting her sent to prison and fall back on a more certain alternative—sending her to her grave instead.

TO BE PROACTIVE, Jordan took a different route each time she went out for her run and found with the bitter cold and sometimes icy or snow-covered streets that she had to abbreviate her runs. Midmorning, she'd scarcely see a soul out and about. No matter which direction she went, though, she always upped her wariness quotient when she approached her house.

Today the streets were still slushy despite having been

plowed. From a couple of blocks away, she recognized Tom walking toward her. Not running—he probably wasn't up to that yet. The stiffness she remembered in his gait was back.

Turn at the corner and circle around to approach the house from the other direction? No, she decided. She'd just ignore him.

Sure, because being snubbed by *her* would deeply wound him. She grimaced, then forgot Tom at the uneasy realization that a vehicle was coming up behind her. A glance over her shoulder told it was a pickup truck she didn't recognize.

She wasn't half a block away from Tom when the truck came even with her, then swerved and braked in her way. She scrambled a couple of steps back. The driver's-side window rolled down, and she saw Steve's brother for the first time since he confronted her after she got out of the hospital.

His expression was as ugly as she would have expected. "Well, well. Mom was right. Here you are."

He had a friend with him—Ryan Carpenter, teammate of Steve's and, later, one of the buddies he frequently met at taverns several nights a week. Leaving her, of course, behind. At first, she'd been hurt, later grateful for the time to herself.

Ryan glared at her, and for a moment she gave herself the luxury of glaring right back.

Not wanting to give them the satisfaction of any other reaction, she spun to circle behind the truck.

Kevin slammed it into Reverse, and it skidded back. Jordan had to dodge, slipping as she did and barely staying on her feet.

She pulled her phone from her pocket. "I'll call 911."

"'Cuz the cops are your best friends," he sneered. "Just what did you do for them when they hauled you in? Has to be some reason they can't see what's in front of their faces."

She would not engage with him. She turned again, this time toward the sidewalk. The truck rolled forward again to cut her off.

Another man called sharply, "What's going on?"

Relief swelled in her. Tom. She'd forgotten he was so close and coming this way. Stepping off the sidewalk, he flicked a glance at her. "Called 911 yet?"

She lied, "Yes."

Kevin looked angry. "We're just having a little talk. This is my sister-in-law. None of your business."

"I'm making it my business," Tom said with an assuredness they lacked. "What I saw is harassment edging toward assault. If she'd fallen when you backed this truck toward her—"

"Took you a while to get here, didn't it? What's the matter?" Kevin's gaze raked him as he mocked, "Did someone *hurt* you?"

Tom gazed calmly back but didn't sound as stunned as she felt. "Interesting you know that's exactly what happened. You wouldn't have had anything to do with it, would you?"

Ryan muttered, "We should get out of here."

"This guy deserves to be taken down a notch." Kevin started to push the driver's-side door open.

Tom stepped forward and with a slap of his hand slammed the door, then reached through the open window and grabbed a fistful of Kevin's coat and shirt right at his throat. "I'm faster and smarter than you are, and don't forget it." He still sounded unnaturally calm. "Now, I think your friend has the right idea."

The hate on Kevin's face eclipsed even the way his mother had looked at Jordan. She stepped back involuntarily.

The next second, Kevin jerked the gearshift into Drive

and stepped on the gas. The truck shot forward, rocked and slithered as he swerved to avoid a parked car, and spat dirty slush back at Tom and Jordan.

Tom looked at her, his eyes not at all calm. "I don't hear a siren."

"I didn't finish the call. After you arrived, I figured you could deal with him. You're a cop, after all."

The muscles in his jaw bunched. "Good thing for you, too."

"Is it?" She started to turn away, but he grabbed her arm.

"Wait. I need to talk to you."

"I've talked to almost everyone in your department." Her expression was as devastated as any he'd seen on her face. "I'm done."

"I'm trying to keep you safe," he said to her back.

He might as well have ignited an explosion.

Chapter Fourteen

"Safe?" Blazing angry now, she swung back to face him. "Is that what you call being handcuffed, knocked down, shoved into a police car? That's the least safe I've ever felt!"

"What?" His eyes darkened as he focused on her cheek and jaw. The scrapes were mostly healed, but the bruising lingered like a yellow stain. "How did that happen?"

She wanted to stay mad, but his obvious outrage made that hard. "Did I mention 'knocked down'?"

"Who did that?"

"An officer who never introduced himself. I was more focused on the gun he was pointing at me than seeing his name tag."

Tom growled an obscenity, thrust his fingers into his hair and yanked. "What were they *thinking*?"

"Same thing you think." A harsh reminder. Still...she owed him for what he'd just done. "Thank you for...intervening. I mean, with Kevin. But I need to get home."

"I'll walk with you."

She had to cool down anyway after standing here so long. "Fine."

Despite obvious pain, Tom stretched his legs to match her speed.

"They said you were shot," she said after a moment.

"Shoulder." He touched his fingers to what must be

his wound beneath the parka. "Less serious wound to my thigh."

"I'm sorry."

Those turbulent eyes met hers. "Not your fault."

"But it is!" she cried. "Some way, somehow, it has to be."

"You need to know that you're no longer considered a suspect for Pete Shroder's murder."

She stopped.

"I talked to one of the detectives in Walla Walla." He told her about the fingerprint, such a small thing, that identified one of the burglars.

Not sure what she felt about news that would have been earthshaking if not for the other attacks, Jordan resumed walking.

"Who was the other guy in the truck?" Tom asked.

Switching gears took her a minute. "A friend of Steve's. One of his closest friends. Ryan Carpenter."

"Huh. Not quite the hothead Kevin is."

She fixed her eyes on her mother's house, half a block ahead. Almost there, thank goodness.

"Kevin implied that he'd just heard from his mother that I'm back in town. She and I met in the grocery store. But he couldn't have missed hearing about the vandalism."

Tom frowned. "No."

"What did you want to talk to me about?"

"I had an idea I just discussed with Guthrie. There's a big downside to it, though."

Jordan stopped where she was on the sidewalk, free of snow because several men on the block regularly came out with their shovels the minute a few flakes fell. "What?" she asked apprehensively. How could her life get *worse*?

He told her, and she immediately saw what he meant by downside. *She* would become the target if the murderer was made to believe that, after his attacks on three men associated with her, the cops *still* refused to believe she might be guilty.

Feeling lightheaded, she realized she'd quit breathing and made herself start up again. "But... Mom. She's so vulnerable."

"Jordan," Tom said quietly, "I mean it when I say your safety *and* your mother's is my number one priority."

Why was she even listening to this? She squared her shoulders. "I told you I wouldn't believe a word you said again, didn't I? I'll buy a gun. Keep myself *and* Mom safe." She walked away, not hearing the crunch of his footsteps behind her.

Then she had a thought. Would a gun shop sell one to her after she'd shot and killed her husband, even if the police labeled the act justified?

She quaked, glad Tom wouldn't be able to tell from behind. She was the one to lie to him now; she never, *never* wanted to touch a gun again.

NOT UNEXPECTEDLY, Guthrie didn't entirely buy into Tom's theory, but he did concede that eliminating Jordan from Shroder's murder introduced some doubt.

With Tom having nixed any more meetings, this conversation was taking place on the phone. He stayed silent, letting Guthrie think.

"Okay," he said finally. "It's worth a try. As often as reporters get in our way, it'll be good to manipulate them for a change."

"You'll handle it?" Tom asked.

"They're used to me giving the press conferences, so yes."

Tom had watched clips of a couple of those press conferences before he accepted the job here. They were pretty

standard for small towns or rural counties: the sheriff behind the mic, a couple of other uniformed officers at his
back to emphasize his authority.

The two men talked for another ten minutes, pinning
down exactly what they wanted to see in print and on the
news.

"We'll do our best to get TV here as well as print reporters. We catch the interest of stations out of Coeur d'Alene,
Moscow, even Missoula or Spokane on a rare occasion. A
follow-up on the shocking, unsolved murder of a respected
ER doc who worked at a regional hospital might do it."

"I want to look at vacation and leave times for last summer for everyone in the department." Guthrie had dodged
Tom's previous demand. "Unexplained absences."

"Why would you be arrowing in on other cops?" The
chief sounded genuinely puzzled—or he was a hell of an
actor.

Tom explained why. "Some of the obvious suspects don't
strike me as patient or organized enough to plan, wait for
the perfect moment and leave such clean crime scenes."
He'd said this before, but the chief didn't want to hear it.
"There may have been friends of Steve's or the family who
got taken on at other departments. We can pursue that. But
first, this is a small town. You could well be unaware of
officers in your department who have a connection to the
Dunn family. I'd like to be sure Bussert wasn't out of town
the week leading up to the Fourth of July, for example."

This silence told him the answer before the chief said
reluctantly, "He was on vacation. A couple other members
of the department were, too. For people with families, it's
natural to want time off around the holiday."

A couple other members.

"Who else?" Tom hoped he sounded as grim as he felt.

Guthrie named two young officers whose names hadn't caught Tom's attention before. "Bowen, too," he threw out with more reluctance.

"He has a wife and kids?"

"Ah, no. Lost his wife a little over a year ago. Freak thing. They'd never had kids. Wasn't himself for a while. Thought he needed some time."

Tom had already felt uneasy about Ronald Bowen without quite being sure why. Maybe he just hadn't liked what he'd seen and heard about the guy's attitude toward Jordan. That could be his usual style—intimidate anyone he interviewed—but there could be something personal, too.

Bussert's feelings for Jordan were definitely personal.

By evening, Tom was second-guessing himself. Had he just painted a target on Jordan?

Wasn't that the point?

Keeping her safe was his number one priority. How was he supposed to do that? Did he start patrolling around Jordan's house from dusk until dawn? Doable, except the intermittent snowfall was a problem, given that footsteps in it would be all too obvious. Also…reluctant as he was to admit it, that was an arduous schedule and activity for a man now recuperating from two separate shootings. Would Guthrie lend him someone? Could he trust that someone?

What Tom wanted was to be inside the Hendrick house. If he could achieve that, he'd have a lot more confidence in his ability to protect Jordan and her mother. Maybe once she saw the newspaper or the press conference on some local TV station, she'd give in.

He grimaced. Pride was a powerful force. He'd betrayed her trust, and he didn't see her forgiving that.

Once he'd checked all his locks and set his handgun on the bedside table, Tom lay back against his pillows, feeling

residual pain in every single one of the places on his body
that had taken bullets. Worse was the sick fear that he'd
screwed up. He should have made a protection detail for
Jordan a requirement for this plan, but he'd been too cocky.
He could keep her safe.

What if he couldn't?

AFTER A LOUSY night's sleep, he called Jordan. Repeatedly.
She didn't answer.

He talked to Guthrie again. Clearly he wasn't the chief's
favorite person anymore. That man eventually growled,
"I'll see what I can come up with. You know what a small
department I have. Adding you to the payroll when you're
not contributing day to day is straining my budget already."

Tom wouldn't have been surprised if one of his molars
cracked.

Nonetheless, the chief pulled off the press conference,
although attendance wasn't what he'd hoped to see. Tom
didn't give a damn; this killer didn't live in Spokane or even
Coeur d'Alene. He or she lived right here in Storm Lake.
Tom would bet on it.

He watched the sheriff giving his statement online. He
appeared deeply concerned and sincere. When the reporter
from the local paper asked about the suspect he understood
had been taken into the station for questioning—he was
careful not to name her, Tom noted—the sheriff managed
to look earnest and regretful.

"That was someone we had to look at, but there was a
solid alibi. I can't say more than that."

A couple more questions followed, mostly interested in
future steps in the investigation. Might the chief request
assistance from the Idaho State Police Investigations?

Guthrie dismissed the question with a curt, "We're not at that point yet."

Tom tried to picture the people on his suspect list—almost all men—watching the nightly local news. He also wondered how much the chief had confided in his second-in-command.

He took a late-afternoon-into-evening nap, then spent the night sitting by his front window, staying alert. His instinct said this was too soon for the killer to make a move, but his gut roiled at the same time with the fear that he was wrong along with the knowledge that someone could slip into the back of the Hendrick house entirely unseen.

The article appeared the next day on the front page above the fold in the skimpy daily newspaper. The headline: No Suspect in Doctor's Murder. Tom winced, but read on. The body of the article might have been written using his script as an outline. He was both satisfied and unnerved. The implication was clear: police no longer suspected Jordan Hendrick...even though that wasn't actually true.

It seemed to Tom that the killer had a couple of best options.

One: murder someone else linked to Jordan, and this time make sure there'd be evidence of her presence at the scene. The problem there was she'd been careful to keep to herself since the doctor was killed—with the exception of Tom. Knowing now that Tom was armed, would the perpetrator try for him again? Was there any chance the perpetrator knew he was a cop? Guthrie had sworn to keep quiet, but who knew?

Two: go for Jordan. Tom liked that option the least, even though he had set it up himself.

Was Jordan really so stubborn she'd go it alone? Even

risk her mother's safety? He hoped not, since he had a plan to ensure Mrs. Hendrick was safeguarded.

Maybe he should buy a down sleeping bag and start camping out on her front porch nights. Wouldn't help if someone broke into the back of the house...except he'd be close enough to hear wood or glass breaking.

"Jordan? Is that you?"

Uh-oh. Jordan had been trying to be so quiet. Mom had read the article in Wednesday's *Storm Lake Tribune* and had been relieved that "those police officers" had finally come to their senses. How could they have thought for a minute that Jordan was capable of such awful things? Jordan had managed to smile, pat her mother's hand and say, "I just hope they figure out who killed Dr. Parnell soon. He was a really nice man who dedicated his life to saving other people."

Mom agreed and had seemingly put the whole thing out of her mind. She'd started browsing gardening magazines and catalogs that showed up in the mailbox, planning orders for new hybrids. Mom found the local nursery to be disappointing since it carried only the usual standbys. Her optimism in planning for spring lifted Jordan's spirits, too, especially since Mom had made such significant strides to full recovery.

Her own worries about the effect stress might have on Mom seemed like a good excuse to keep her intense anxiety to herself. That she spent half her nights creeping through the house, listening for any sound that didn't belong, wasn't something she wanted to share with her mother.

But apparently the floorboard had creaked.

"It's just me, Mom," she said. "I'm sorry if I woke you."

Her mother's voice carried from the bedroom. "What *are* you doing?"

"Oh, I—" Cell phone, that was it. "I think I left my phone in the kitchen, and I need to charge it."

"You've been sneaking around for the last half hour," Mom said tartly.

The few times Jordan had tried to sneak out of the house as a teenager, her mother had caught her. Why had she assumed a stroke diminished Mom's excellent hearing? She sighed.

It was weird talking in the darkness. "I'm having insomnia, and I keep thinking of things to fuss about, that's all."

"You think someone's going to do something else like the vandalism, don't you?"

"I guess that scares me a little," she admitted. A lot, actually, since it wasn't anything as innocuous as spray paint that worried her.

"I wish you would talk to Tom. He was so kind and helpful. I don't understand why you've cut him off."

Mouth open as she tried to come up with a believable excuse, she was suddenly hit by the realization that she'd underestimated her mother's acuity. Clearly, Mom had a lot better idea of what was going on than Jordan had wanted to believe. A stroke could cause cognitive damage, but there'd been no indication it had in Mom's case. The difficulty with forming words wasn't the same thing.

"I'm turning the hall light on," Jordan said. She followed the rectangle of light into the bedroom and sat at the edge of her mother's bed. Mom reached out and took her hand in a surprisingly firm grip.

"I...thought he was becoming a friend," Jordan said. "Maybe—"

"Even more?"

"Yeah. Then I overheard him talking to the police chief and learned that he'd been pretending all that time so he could get close to me. They did think I could have committed murder." She swallowed. "Tom is a cop, Mom. A police detective. He was hired to cozy up to me and catch me red-handed." That implied bloodstained hands, didn't it? She shivered.

"Are you sure?" her mother whispered, her fingers tightening on Jordan's.

"He admitted it."

Mom stayed quiet for a minute, then said, "Does he still believe you could have killed someone?"

"He claims he doesn't, but how can I believe him? He lied about everything."

"I saw the way he looked at you. Is it possible he started by doing his job, but also came to care about you?"

"How am I supposed to know?" Jordan asked simply.

"Maybe…you have to go with your instinct."

Like you did with Dad? Jordan wanted to ask, but that would have been cruel. They never talked about her father.

"I've always worried," Mom said softly, scarcely any slur in her voice. "After your father left, you changed. I think you've never been able to trust."

"I trusted Steve."

"Did you really? Or were you trying desperately to make a family, because that was something you wanted so much?"

Shocked, Jordan stared at her mother's face. "I…you knew?"

"Of course I knew, but you were so set on marrying him. Nothing I could have said would have stopped you. I just prayed he'd turn into a better man than I feared he was."

"But you were right about him."

"I didn't want to be."

Were those tears trickling down her mother's face? Jordan leaned over and rested her head on her mother's shoulder, accepting comfort she'd denied herself for so long.

"I didn't want to admit that I never let myself see who he really was," she whispered. "I kept thinking if I pretended—"

"It doesn't work that way," her mother said sadly. "I... tried that, too. Eventually I realized that for all the grief I suffered after your father left, he'd given me more joy. You."

Jordan lifted her head slightly so she could see Mom's smile.

Jordan cried, and knew as her mother cradled her, she was doing the same.

She sat there a long time, until she was sure Mom slept. Then she got up, turned off the hall light, waited until her eyes adjusted to the darkness, and crept to the living room so she could peer out the front.

Nothing was moving. No light shone in Tom's house. Was he awake, too? Watching? Afraid for her?

What did her instinct say about him?

Chapter Fifteen

Two days after the press conference, Tom accepted how much he hated his current role, and decided the time had come to shed it.

He started by crossing the street and ringing Jordan's doorbell. A car he recognized was parked at the curb, which told him a therapist of some kind or other was here keeping Jordan's mother occupied. He couldn't be positive that Jordan hadn't slipped out the back for one of her risky solitary runs, but—

Wearing skinny jeans, clogs and a sweater that hung to mid-thigh, her hair in a high ponytail, Jordan opened the door. She'd never looked more beautiful to him even though he saw no welcome on her face. Instead, she gazed at him in astonishment. "Really? You can't take a hint, or ten?"

"Please," he said, sticking out a booted foot so she couldn't slam the door. "I need to talk to you."

Tiny furrows formed on her usually smooth forehead. He still couldn't tell what she was thinking, but some emotion had momentarily darkened her eyes. Whatever it was, she chose to step back so he could enter, although she sounded distinctly sardonic when she said, "Disturbed that your plan hasn't worked?"

His plan. To goad a cold-blooded killer to go after *her*.

"Yes and no," he said. "I've been watching. I'm the one

getting impatient even though I didn't expect immediate action."

"Why?" She waved him to the couch and sat down in an easy chair.

"Because he follows his rules. You have to go out with a man—normally twice—before he acts."

She gazed at him expressionlessly. "Except for you."

"It may have become apparent to him—I say *him* for convenience's sake—that you were unlikely to date a man anytime in the next decade or two. *Especially* while you were in Storm Lake."

"I didn't date you at all."

"We spent quite a bit of time together. Running, at the hospital…and kissing."

"We kissed once." Each word froze into an icicle.

"We did. In plain sight."

Her eyes narrowed to slits. "Like you planned."

"No—"

She went on as if he hadn't opened his mouth. "So this guy was eager to go for it, but when that was a flop, he decided to be…patient?" Her eyebrows had a quirk to them.

The muscles in his jaw flexed. "I've decided I need to investigate, not keep sitting around waiting for another attack on me, or one on you."

Jordan just waited.

He pulled his phone out of his pocket, called up his list of suspects, and said, "I want you to talk to me about these people. Whatever comes to you."

She closed her eyes momentarily, then said, "All right."

He started with the women: Steve Dunn's mother and sister, and a former girlfriend who'd gotten the boot when he became interested in Jordan.

"Kendra Gruener? I can't imagine. I mean, they were

only sophomores when they dated for a few months. She should be grateful she *didn't* stay with him."

"She should, but that doesn't mean she is."

Jordan sat thinking about it for a minute. "I don't think it can be Kendra. She was shy. I heard her dad was an alcoholic and her family life was a mess."

"Making her vulnerable," Tom said slowly.

"Right." She opened her mouth, then closed it. Had she been about to admit the monster she'd married had chosen her, if only subconsciously, for the same reason? Too bad Dunn couldn't see the gutsy woman she'd become, the one who'd had no problem holding off the cop who'd lied to her.

"Any suggestion he had an affair?"

Jordan shook her head decisively. "I can't swear one of those nights he was out at the tavern he didn't take a woman in back, but I don't think so." She focused again on his list. "Steve's mother... She hates me. She, um, thinks it's my fault he didn't go to college and continue his glorious football career, because she can't blame *him* for anything. I ran into her at the grocery store not long ago. Did I tell you? I pointed out that she had to know what Steve was, that I was willing to bet he'd learned from his father and that *she* knew what being married to an abusive man was like. I'm pretty sure from her expression I was right. I felt hateful for reminding her."

In retrospect, the sister reminded her a little of herself, too. "She almost seemed...skittish around Steve. Trying to please him, you know?"

"Kevin?"

Jordan frowned. "They weren't the kind of family that held Sunday dinners. And with him the youngest... I didn't see them together that often."

When prodded, she gave impressions of Steve Dunn's

friends. Most, she thought, hung around him for the re-flected glory. He had her study the list again to trigger memories. She knocked some names off his list. One guy had gotten a full ride to college with a baseball scholarship; another had moved away and died in a motorcycle accident. One lived in town, but was working with his dad in an auto repair business and doing some custom paint jobs on the side. Married, too, according to Mom, with at least one kid.

Cody Bussert, she'd disliked intensely. "After Colin—Dr. Parnell—was found dead and Cody came to the house, I could see he *wanted* to blame me."

"Or to make sure you were blamed?"

Jordan bit her lip. "Maybe. His level of anger didn't make sense after all these years. I mean, Steve and he were friends, but…"

"Unless Steve had done something extraordinary for him. I hear Cody's family was seriously troubled, too."

"Yes, I vaguely remember that he went to juvie for a while, but what could Steve have done to earn loyalty so strong, Cody would kill innocent people to get revenge on me?"

That was the problem, wasn't it? The motivation was so damned twisted, Tom had trouble assigning it to anyone, even the brother, who had earned a spot at the top of his list after the way he looked at Jordan the day he confronted her.

"Kevin," she said, reverting to the brother. "He desper-ately wanted to *be* like Steve. I used to wonder if Steve had stood up to his dad for his little brother. Maybe took some blows for Kevin's sake." Her eyes met Tom's with sudden alarm. "I don't know anything like that. I'm not even sure their father was abusive. I…guessed. That's all."

"What happened to the father?" Now, if *he'd* still been alive…

"Killed himself and another motorist when he was driving drunk. I saw him at games, and around, but he died when Steve and I were seniors, so I never met him." She wrapped her arms around herself.

Comforting herself? Tom wondered.

"Steve blew up because his father was being blamed. He insisted the other driver must have flashed her brights at him or something like that. Couldn't have been the booze. Didn't matter how much he had to drink, he was a good driver."

"Lot of denial in that family," Tom commented.

Jordan's crooked smile was sad enough to perturb him. "I guess it was contagious."

Or her own SOB of a father had damaged her as much as an abusive drunkard had his family.

There were a couple of other names they discussed that Jordan seemed more uncertain about. Tom mentally shifted them to his B list.

He tried to sound offhanded when he asked about Deputy Chief Bowen. "Sounds like he's given you a hard time."

"He shouldn't have been allowed to be part of the investigation," she said, instantly angry. "But I suppose the department is too small to rule out two officers."

Tom stiffened. "Why shouldn't he have?"

"He was around back then. Steve called him Uncle Ronnie. I'm not sure whether there's really a blood relationship, or whether he and Steve's dad were friends. Steve and he talked pretty often, and they went hunting and camping together a few times while we were married. I'd see him out by his truck when he picked Steve up, but he never came to the door and we never had anything I'd call a conversation."

Tom had some incredulous and profane thoughts. *Knowing* the guy had that kind of relationship with Jordan's dead husband, Guthrie had still thought it was fine and dandy to let him be involved in an investigation into her possible complicity in two murders?

That said, the guy had been a cop for a lot of years. His promotion to second-in-command suggested that he hadn't had uncontrollable anger management issues. How likely was it that he'd go off the deep end now?

Still, Tom couldn't believe the chief had been shielding an officer and maybe old friend. Maybe going so far as to steer the investigation to Jordan to be sure no one looked at his deputy chief?

If all of this been conscious on Guthrie's part, he needed to be fired—probably along with Bussert and Bowen. If that happened, Tom wouldn't be real popular in this department. Right now, he had one reason why he'd consider sticking to the Storm Lake PD after this was over: Jordan.

He didn't say any of that to her, but he moved Bowen up to his A list. Kevin Dunn was still up there, but their one encounter had introduced some real doubt into his mind. Was the guy capable of being coolheaded enough to pull off these murders? Bussert was still an unknown. Bowen, though, had experience and an ego on display. He was capable of the planning and execution of these crimes. Didn't mean he'd done it; even if he'd had a warm relationship with a real or surrogate nephew, why would he harbor so much rage over the course of years?

Still, a scenario was already playing out in Tom's head. What if Steve's mother told Bowen to butt out? Hadn't she implied that? Carolyn married and started her own family. Maybe Kevin was too angry to turn to his uncle. But there was Steve, the golden boy, the son Ronnie hadn't had.

And what if there was some guilt because Ronnie hadn't stepped in soon enough to keep Steve from sharing his fa-

ther's anger and brutality? Hard to accept your own failing, Tom thought. But there was Jordan, who'd killed Steve.
Blame *her*.

It made sense, even if Tom had just made the whole
thing up.

Finally, he said, "I'm going to track everyone down. Find
out where they are now, where they were when the doctor was killed, and where they were on the Fourth of July.
Were any of them footloose enough to be able to go to Walla
Walla for a few days or a week without anyone noticing?"
He didn't mention that he already knew two of the people
they'd discussed had in fact been free and unaccounted for
that weekend.

"Kevin's married."

"Appears his wife left him. Don't know exactly when
yet, but last summer. He lost his job about the same time—
bad attitude, not his work ethic—and that could have triggered him to want to blame you for all his woes." Would
have left him free for a side trip to Walla Walla, too.

For a moment, they just looked at each other. "Thank
you," he said. "For talking to me."

"I should have done it sooner."

He tucked away his phone and rose to his feet, gazing
down at her. "Do you know how much I hate nights? Knowing by the time I hear or see something, I could be too late?"

She gave him a wild look, then bowed her head for a
moment, letting him see the fragile vertebrae on her nape.
"I...didn't try to buy a gun."

He didn't know whether to be glad or sorry. The idea of
her having to kill somebody, with all the horror that would
stir up, disturbed him almost as much as knowing she and
her mother were defenseless every night.

"I know you're angry with me." He sounded hoarse.

"I don't blame you. But I'd give a lot to spend nights over here. I could bunk down on the couch. You'd barely know I'm here."

"I can't remember the last time I really slept." She gripped one hand with the other, white-knuckling it. "I keep thinking, pride goeth before a fall."

When Jordan paused, he quit breathing.

With the faintest tremor in her voice, she said, "I don't want to fall. And especially…"

She was afraid of anything happening to her mother.

Exultation ripped through him. She hadn't forgiven him…but she'd taken the first step.

Plus, once he introduced his plan to get her mother out of the house, Jordan embraced it. Mom was going to have a fake crisis and be transported to the hospital, after which she'd be shifted to the rehab facility where she'd been before. She could continue to get therapy there. He'd made calls today to arrange all this—subject to Jordan and her mother's agreement. Tom was careful not to let her guess how much fast-talking he'd had to do to set this up. It might have been impossible if he hadn't encountered such fondness for Shelly Hendrick and her daughter. Plus, he'd been able to use Dr. Parnell's name.

It was hard to keep his hands to himself when he saw the relief on her face. "I'll persuade her." She met his eyes. "Thank you."

LATE AFTERNOON, Tom called. After she said hello, there was a long pause. "You answered," he said finally.

"I let you in the house," she pointed out.

"Not necessarily the same thing. Ah…be ready for the ambulance. Probably another hour or two. I'll make sure I'm not around. Better if you look scared and on your own."

Jordan agreed.

The whole operation went incredibly smoothly. Mom obligingly helped the two medics settle her onto a gurney. Jordan ran outside holding Mom's hand and watched as she was loaded into the back of the ambulance. The male medic winked at Jordan, who tried to sound frantic. "I'll follow you to the hospital."

Mom barely paused in the ER, where a clearly complicit doctor immediately admitted her. Had Tom gained so much cooperation because hospital personnel were angry and grieving about Colin Parnell's death? Did the administration know what was happening?

After sitting with Mom, she left to be home in time for dinner and to take half a dozen calls from friends of her mother and neighbors who had heard about the new crisis. She assured them that Mom was doing fine; it had just been a scare, but the doctor wanted her to spend a few days in rehab again where she could be watched closely. Nobody asked her to detail exactly what symptoms had led to the supposed 911 call.

Tom had let her know that he planned to slink through a few backyards well after dark and get to her house without openly crossing the street. Hearing no sounds out of the ordinary, Jordan waited at the kitchen table for his knock on the back door. She couldn't concentrate enough to browse news online or read. It was the first time she'd let herself fully realize that all of this had been designed to leave her ostensibly alone.

No, *really* alone for a good part of the day.

She thought about getting out a blanket and comforter and a pillow and piling them on the sofa to make it obvious where she expected him to sleep, except then it occurred to her that maybe he'd want Mom's bed so someone breaking in didn't see him right away. She plopped back down at the table.

He didn't rap lightly until almost nine o'clock. When she let him in, he asked how the transfer to the hospital had gone today.

"Like clockwork," she admitted. "I don't know how you talked so many people into cooperating. I mean, she's taking up a hospital bed tonight that somebody else might need!"

Tom smiled. "No, they have plenty of room right now. Everybody there knows your mother. They'd do anything for her."

That made Jordan's eyes sting. This was all so elaborate, it was hard to see how it could be a ploy to catch her in the act. Yet whatever her instincts insisted, she hadn't a hundred percent settled into believing he had faith in her innocence and really was here for her.

"I'm so grateful. I guess you figured out that right now, Mom's my weakness. If somebody hurt her…"

"Hey. Let's go sit in the living room."

She nodded. Tom checked the blinds to be sure they were all closed before he sat down with a sigh, stretched out his legs and patted the sofa cushion beside him.

Too close to him. She perched in the wing chair.

He watched her thoughtfully, except that wasn't entirely it. Her fingernails bit into her palms. Okay, thoughtful might be right, except she'd never had anybody focus on her so relentlessly. And *what* he was thinking so hard about was open to question.

She scrambled for something to say. "Did you learn anything today?"

"I talked to Kevin's ex-wife. She left him a few weeks before the Fourth, and says he got canned from his latest roofing job right before that. She said she'd had enough. She agreed he hates you but says he doesn't use a computer much. She can't picture him following you online long-term."

She blinked. "I guess that's what happened."

"Given that you lived in a different state, nobody from back home just stumbled on an article about Shroder's murder and your association with him."

"I didn't have—"

"You had enough to merit a visit from a detective," he said grimly. "And potentially to provide a model for future killings."

Jordan found herself curling forward. "But three years later?"

He leaned toward her, any suggestion that he was relaxed gone. "Here's what I think happened. I think the killer *was* following you online. Could have been only occasional. Maybe he just hoped to find out you'd been killed in a car accident, or murdered a second husband and were in jail. He wasn't really motivated to take action until some bad stuff happened in the late spring or early summer. Whatever it was, that was the trigger. He couldn't fix his marriage or bring his wife back to life or time travel so he wasn't fired, but *you* gave him a focus for all his rage and grief."

He'd explained this before, without mentioning the trigger part. Shivering, she almost wished he hadn't been so graphic. "Bad stuff," she murmured.

"I have some doubts about Kevin, but he fits the pattern in a lot of ways. Job loss, wife leaves him, he's feeling humiliated, powerless, and his big brother isn't around anymore to shore up his ego."

"If Steve ever did," she mumbled. "I heard him be really sharp with his mother, but Kevin…maybe that was different. They were close."

"Did Kevin go hunting with Uncle Ronnie, too?"

"I don't know."

His jaw set before he added, "Carolyn says Bowen really was Steve's uncle, her mother's brother. She remembers him being nice when she was little, but he and the dad clashed. She thinks he might not have been that welcome."

"Clashed. Like two bulls?"

Tom grinned. "Ronnie didn't have his own herd, so maybe he was getting a little too possessive with another man's."

"But what does that have to do with *me*?" Except she knew. She did. She'd killed Steve, the shining boy.

Back to that watchful thing, Tom said, "Bowen took his own hit not that long before the Fourth of July. His wife died. Guthrie called it a freak accident. She fell down a flight of steps into the basement of their home. What if she was pushed?"

"You mean, he was abusive, too." Her stomach had tied itself into knots. If she'd known more about Steve's family, would she have married him however excited she'd been by his attention?

"No domestic violence calls, so I can't say. Either way, with Steve gone, too, he was suddenly left alone."

"Does Bowen know you're a cop?"

"If he didn't, he does now. Everyone will be talking. Whether Guthrie opened his mouth sooner… I don't know." He sighed and, as if he'd said all he intended to, he lifted his arms above his head and stretched. Winced, too, as if he'd forgotten his newly wounded shoulder wasn't going to cooperate and he wasn't as limber as he thought he was.

"I'll get you some bedding. Unless you want Mom's room?"

"No, the couch is fine."

It didn't take her a minute to produce a pillow and a couple of blankets. Then, hovering, she said, "I should think about bed, too. Do you plan to slip out early tomorrow?"

"Yeah."

"Okay." Jordan let herself look at him, really look, and said shakily, "I'm glad you're here. Thank you."

She was ready to flee when he rose to his feet and said abruptly, "You may never believe me, but…I didn't kiss you as part of the act."

Chapter Sixteen

He hadn't meant to open his mouth.

Jordan looked as stunned as he felt. "You bragged to him. I heard you."

"I know. I can't even explain. I was ashamed the minute the words left my mouth. Kissing you for the first time... it should have stayed private. You have to know I've been drawn to you since our first meeting. Not until after it happened did I realize it was a good setup if the right person had seen us."

"I wish I *could* believe you," she whispered.

"You can," he said hoarsely. "About this. I swear." What he wanted was to reach for her, but instead he didn't dare move.

She pressed her lips together, hesitating while he held his breath. This was like being back in junior high when you thought your life would end if she said, *Get lost*.

Only...she didn't. She took the smallest of steps forward and said in that same, soft voice, "It just happened for me, too. I should never have let myself even think about a man like that, only there you were."

"Will you let me kiss you again? Nobody can see us." Had he ever begged a woman in his life? He was pretty sure not, but that's what he was doing now. What he was asking for was a level of trust, and they both knew it.

Jordan gave a tiny nod and stepped forward. With a groan, he engulfed her in his arms and kissed her with ravaging hunger and very little tenderness. She whimpered, threw her arms around his neck and kissed him back as if she was as hungry for this as he was. As if she'd lain awake nights aching because she couldn't quit thinking about him.

He broke off long enough for them both to suck in air, then nipped her earlobe. "God, Jordan. I've been so afraid…"

The kisses got deeper, more passionate. Somehow he'd sprawled back on the sofa with Jordan straddling his lap. He pushed his hands up inside her shirt and under her bra, groaning at the feel of firm, ripe flesh topped by hard nipples.

"I have to see you." He was in the act of ripping her shirt over her head when he felt her stiffen.

"Wait!"

Wait? He was dying here.

"This is…awfully fast." She sounded as agonized as he felt, but she went on, "Hearing what you said to the chief… That *hurt*."

Because she'd been falling for him, the way he was for her.

But there was another reason she was right. This wasn't a good idea. He had a disquieting memory of that other kiss, when he'd been utterly—and, as it turned out, almost fatally—unaware of what was happening around them.

Easing his hands from beneath her bra, sliding them down her slim belly, he tugged her down to rest her forehead on his. "Once I get my hands on you, I get distracted. I'm supposed to stay alert."

Tom knew he shouldn't make love with this woman now that their trap had been set, not the way he wanted to. "God, I don't want to let you go."

"I know." She kissed his neck, then climbed off him as he pried his fingers from her butt and nape. Her lips were puffy, one cheek red from the stubble on his jaw, but a hint of her wariness had returned.

She'd been right to put on the brakes. If they made love, it might kill him to see that expression in her eyes again.

But what did he do but blurt, "I've never felt anything like this before." Yeah, that was it; roll over and expose his bare belly.

Her face softened, but what she said was, "I…haven't either. But…I swore I'd never let myself be that vulnerable to a man again. You reinforced my vow when you lied to me."

"You're saying you can't get over that."

"No." She apparently tried to smile, but it didn't fly. "Just…asking you to be patient."

He took some deep breaths. There was only one answer. "I can do that. Whatever you need. However long you need."

Her lips trembled, her eyes shimmered, and she said, "Thank you," before backing away. It was all he could do not to stop her.

Tom could hardly wait for his night on the too-short sofa while living with the knowledge that she was only a couple of rooms away.

A DETECTIVE'S TOOL kit included the ability to stay calm and outwardly nonjudgmental. Tom didn't remember ever struggling the way he was while he listened to that jackass Kevin Dunn explain why he hated Jordan Hendrick.

"Isn't 'obeying' part of the wedding vow? Steve let her get by with not taking his name, and what's that say about her? What kind of marriage is it when she's defying her husband before the ring's on her finger?"

"Your wife seems to have gone back to her maiden name," he observed mildly.

Kevin sneered. "She knows she won't get a second chance with me!"

The two men stood on the porch of the shabby house Kevin rented. Both kept their hands in their pockets and thanks to the cold were puffing white clouds as if they were sucking on cigarettes between every breath. Kevin hadn't issued an invite for Tom to step into his place. Tom preferred to stay in the open.

He pointed out that every cop and medic who saw the scene after Jordan shot Steve felt sure she'd made a life-or-death decision.

Kevin's response was to spit onto the porch boards, just missing Tom's foot. "*Every* cop didn't think that. Probably not every medic, either. Else there wouldn't have been so much talk after."

Tom raised his brows. "Do you know a cop who disagreed?"

"Sure! My uncle Ronnie. He was one of the first guys there."

Actually, he hadn't been a first responder. Interesting that the deputy chief had let Kevin believe he was.

"Looked like a fight to him," Kevin claimed, "maybe both of 'em beating on each other, 'til that woman went for Steve's gun."

Tom had to remind himself that Kevin may have heard what he wanted to hear from Bowen. Nothing in the police reports indicated any such opinion.

Kevin continued to spew his vitriol, insisting, "A guy's got a right to know what his wife is up to. Don't seem like too much to ask."

Tom's jaw had begun to ache with the effort of holding

back. Even now, he stuck with conversational, not necessarily disagreeing with this SOB. "I understand he lost his
job that day. Went home steaming."

The sneer was imprinting itself on Kevin's face, the lines
deep. There'd come a day when he wouldn't be able to erase
the expression. "Who's to say *she* wasn't the one got mad
because they might have to tighten their belts a little? He
didn't like that job anyway. He'd have done better, but I
guess she didn't believe that."

After another five or ten minutes, Tom worked his way
around to asking whether Kevin had ever wondered where
she was or what she was doing after she recovered and made
the decision to leave town.

He shrugged. "Didn't have to."

"Because?"

For the first time, he displayed some caution. "I know
people who don't do nothing but follow social media time
wasters."

"Anybody in particular keep you updated?"

"Not one person especially. And I'm done talking to you
now. Uncle Ronnie got to arrest her. He can tell you stuff."

Tom didn't bother to mention that "Ronnie" hadn't actually arrested Jordan, because he'd had no legal justifica-
tion. It was unlikely Bowen had ever actually told Kevin
any such thing. Tom nodded politely enough, and felt sure
Kevin watched as he walked back to his vehicle and drove
away.

His cover was definitely blown now. He was still driving his own SUV, but he'd shown a badge to Kevin, whose
shock had been apparent. Tom had no doubt Kevin was on
the phone with Uncle Ronnie right this minute.

How did Bowen feel about the subterfuge, assuming he

hadn't known about it all along? Hell. Tom had never exchanged a word with the man.

Deciding to tackle Bowen next, he went by the police
station, getting lucky when he saw the man walking across
the parking lot. He didn't see any resemblance to Steve;
Bowen had to have been shorter than both his nephews and
his sister's husband, but was bulked up enough to suggest
he did some weight lifting.

When Tom approached him, Bowen's eyebrows rose.
"Well, aren't you the surprise. I hear Guthrie's letting you
call the shots these days."

Tom held out a hand. "He hired me to initially focus on
the one investigation."

They shook, Bowen not looking happy but not hostile,
either.

"Yeah," he agreed, "Steve Dunn was my nephew. Far as
I saw, he was always a good kid. I thought of him as a son."

"What about Kevin?"

"I offered to give him time, but he tried my patience."
The deputy chief shook his head. "I thought I could get my
sister to leave that SOB she'd married, but she wouldn't
break up her family. Better for everyone if she had."

Tom agreed wholeheartedly but didn't say so.

The two men chatted for a few more minutes. Not so
much as a flicker of response seemed off. If Tom had been
more trusting by nature, he'd have crossed Bowen off his
list. He'd also made note of how much of what the deputy
chief said fitted in perfectly with the scenario Tom had
come up with.

Not needing GPS to find anyplace in a town this size,
he drove to Mama Dunn's place next. She was a cook and
waitress at a truck stop just outside town, and he hadn't
checked on her work schedule, but he found her home.

She even asked him in and offered a cup of coffee, which he declined.

Surprisingly, Nancy Dunn didn't give any sign she knew a thing about Tom beyond his introduction. Certainly not that he'd been in town for a few months now, playing a role. She was a lot more careful in her answers to Tom's questions than her son had been, but she expressed a significant amount of anger at Jordan, too.

The longer they talked, though, the more the anger dwindled into wrenching sadness.

"Steve was a good boy!" Her eyes strayed to the fireplace mantel, where Steve appeared to have received star billing, from a grinning toddler picture through his graduation photo. "Everyone always looked up to him."

"I understand he was a heck of an athlete," Tom remarked, to keep her going. Seeing that row of images, he found himself annoyed again at his private acknowledgment that her oldest son had been an exceptionally good-looking young man. Jordan had had good reason for her attraction.

The father, he noted, had been a big, burly guy, undoubtedly handsome in his day.

No surprise, Mrs. Dunn was a pretty woman for her age. He'd have wondered about why she hadn't remarried had it not been for his memory of Jordan's speculation. If her husband had been as abusive as his son, this woman must, on some level, be rejoicing in the ability to live without fear, without having to worry about pleasing anyone.

He chose to be blunt with her about Jordan's medical records. He started with the ones from the ER across the state border. "The fact that Steve recognized she needed medical care but didn't want her to receive it here in town where he and she were known is a real red flag."

She stared at him, then faltered, "I...I didn't know about that."

Truth or lie?

He laid out what he knew about Jordan's injuries in that final confrontation before saying, "I understand you loved your son, but you must have been aware of his temper."

Her cheeks flushed, a color especially unattractive when accented by the blush she'd applied, but he also saw her grief. "I...knew he could get real mad." More softly, she added, "Like his daddy did. I hoped, well, that he'd never hit a woman, especially one he loved." She looked down at the hands she'd woven together on her lap. "I guess I didn't want to know. Once or twice I didn't like the way he talked to Jordan, but, well, his daddy could be hard on me and the kids, too."

"You put up with it."

He hated to see the shame in the eyes she raised to meet his.

"I was raised to think that's what a woman does. I never could've done what she did." Her hands writhed. "I shouldn't have said what I did to her."

He pretended ignorance. "When was that?"

"Oh, a few times. Right after, and then when we came face-to-face not that long ago. She was doing the right thing, coming home because her mama needed her, and I was downright nasty."

"I suspect she understood," he said gently.

"If...if you talk to her, would you tell her I'm sorry?"

He thought, *Why don't you do that yourself?* but only nodded. "I will."

After giving her a moment to regain her composure, he said, "I get the feeling Kevin and your brother are still fixed on blaming Jordan."

"Steve was...well, you know. Special. The best-looking,

the best athlete this high school has ever had. Kevin wanted to be just like his big brother. Ronnie and I never did get along that well, but I have to give him credit for making himself available to both boys, but especially Steve. When Steve didn't get the kind of football scholarship he wanted, I hoped Ron would talk him into going to the police academy. That would have been a good career for him."

Tom hid a wince. He hoped psychological testing would have eliminated Steve Dunn before he was ever issued a badge.

When he asked about her son's friends, she said, "Oh, there's some who might speak out if they came to run into her, but that's all. Not like they'd attack her or anything."

"You know there's a possibility that a couple of men have been murdered with the intention of making it look like Jordan committed the crimes."

"I heard, but who would do that?" she cried. "No one I know."

He didn't say, *Oh, I'm sure you know someone who has done exactly that.* Instead, he thanked her for her time and went home to make himself lunch.

Somehow, he wasn't at all surprised to hear a deep-throated vehicle approaching entirely too fast and braking hard enough to skid on the icy pavement of his driveway even before he had a chance to heat up the frying pan to grill the cheese sandwiches he put together.

What did surprise him after a prolonged burst of *bongs* from his doorbell was the identity of his visitor. Kevin wasn't the only hothead; Officer Cody "Buzz" Bussert had been shaped by the same cookie cutter.

TOM SHOWED UP substantially earlier that evening, although he had waited until full dark. Still, his knock on the back

door scared Jordan. He'd no sooner stepped inside, closed
and locked the door, than he pulled her into his arms.

"Damn. I sit watching your house from my living room
window *knowing* you could be in trouble, and I wouldn't
know." He pressed a kiss to the top of her head before he
loosened his grip. "I bought some timers for the lights today
if anybody is watching my place. Which I don't expect now
that everyone knows I'm a cop."

No, *she* was the bait.

After a couple of shaky breaths, she recovered her poise.
"Have you had dinner?"

"I did." Without discussion, they went to the living room,
where Tom carefully lowered himself to sit at one end of
the sofa.

Jordan hesitated, then chose the sofa, too, but with a
cushion separating them. "Can you tell me about your day?"

"Normally, I wouldn't," he said bluntly. "There are
things a cop can't disclose. And honestly, when you've seen
terrible things, sometimes you don't want to talk about it.
That…can lead to problems in a relationship."

She nodded her understanding. Being stonewalled by
your husband would be frustrating when you knew he was
open with his coworkers but not you.

He continued, "That said, everything I'm doing right now,
everyone I talk to, has to do with you. You're entitled."

He didn't say, *I know I don't have a hope in hell of gaining your trust if I hold back*, but if what he'd said last night
was true, he had to be thinking that.

Watching her, he moved his shoulders a little, and she
saw a nerve twitch in his cheek. Because he hurt? Was he
doing physical therapy for this new wound? If he wasn't
finding enough time, that *would* be her fault, she thought.

"Did you see Buzz come roaring up to my house?"

"No. Really? I must have been with Mom."

"Oh, yeah. He was mad as hell to find out that his talk with Chief Guthrie—the one I recommended—wasn't a fatherly chat, it was really what Bussert called a grilling. He blamed you, of course. After all, he was embarrassed by getting cut out of any calls or investigations concerned with you. Now he knows it's my fault. That anybody could suggest he'd have murdered complete strangers to get revenge on you shocked him. He's a good cop, and nobody is going to say he isn't. Especially *you*."

She rolled her eyes. "Back to blaming me."

"Yeah, but he resents me, too." He grinned. "Apparently Guthrie left Bussert with the impression that I'm next thing to a cripple, which is fine in case he plans to sneak into my house one of these nights."

"I guess he hasn't seen you running."

He smiled crookedly. "Or maybe he has."

She gave him a reproving look. "You were getting better until you got shot *again*."

"Bussert couldn't believe anyone would look at him for something like that. Yeah, he and Steve were good friends, but I could see some doubt when I laid out the facts for him. I got the impression no one had ever encouraged him to look at your medical records or the photographs from the scene."

His matter-of-fact comment made Jordan want to cringe, although she refused to do so. She was done being ashamed in any way about her brief marriage or its ending. Still, she didn't love the idea that Tom was stirring new talk about her. She could just imagine the whispers. *Do you know how long she was unconscious? I hear she had spiral fractures. Oh, and a broken collarbone, and...* She hated even worse to know police officers like Cody Bussert could look at photos of her, battered and pathetic.

"Has telling people about my medical records changed a single person's mind?" she asked.

"Yeah." His voice dropped to a deep, velvety note. "Steve's mother. She...asked me to tell you she's sorry for the things she said to you."

Jordan held herself very still. "You're serious."

"I am. I think she was sincere."

Having confirmation that "Buzz" Bussert still blamed her for everything up to and including climate change—assuming he believed in that—wasn't even a faint surprise. To know that her ex-mother-in-law had changed her attitude that drastically felt... Wow, Jordan didn't even know.

"Jordan?" Tom asked, in that same tone. One she could almost call tender.

"I think I feel even worse about what I said to her."

He held out a hand. "Any chance I can talk you into scooting over here?"

How could she resist? She wanted to cuddle with him, even if much more than that still scared her. Once she came in reach, he wrapped an arm around her, and she soaked in what she barely recognized as happiness.

Her happiness expanded as Tom talked more about where his investigation had taken him. Detectives Dutton and Shannon had been helping him canvass hotels and Airbnb and vacation rentals in search of any of the names on his list. No luck so far.

"Most of these men would have been fine camping out," he grumbled.

He even talked about his disappointment and anger at Chief Guthrie and Deputy Chief Bowen.

"Should you be telling me things like this?" she asked.

He tipped his head so she could see his smile and the expression in his vividly blue eyes. "Like I said, you're entitled. Besides…"

"You think you have to earn my trust."

"Don't I? But that isn't what I was thinking. I trust you. I'd like to see you less guarded, but no matter what, I know you won't open your mouth when you shouldn't."

The lump in her throat took her aback. Did she really still think he might betray her again—or was she just afraid of taking a risk?

He hadn't known her when he took this job. He was set up to suspect her, and she couldn't blame him for that. But unless the instinct she'd been listening to was completely wrong, he had since shifted to an intense focus on protecting her and finding out the truth, just as he'd promised. Couldn't she forgive him for his initial lies and misdirection?

If what he was implying was true—that he might even be falling in love with her—how could she *not* take the chance?

For all the hurts she'd suffered, the times she'd lost confidence in herself, she felt an unexpected certainty that he was much the same. He'd said enough about his childhood and, more recently, losing his friend, she knew that was true for him, too. They *matched*…if she could erase her last doubts. Or were they fears?

"What are you thinking?" he asked, voice husky.

She couldn't say. Not yet. Her mouth opened, closed, then opened again. "I was conducting an internal debate."

His expression of satisfaction struck her as sexual because he might look like that after—

"So, okay, I was hoping you'd kiss me again."

There was that wicked grin. "Oh, yeah."

Chapter Seventeen

Jordan had never known how much she detested waiting. Funny, when that's what so much of her life had come down to since she raced home to sit, yes, waiting at her mother's side at the hospital. Would she live? Could she recover?

This was as bad. She'd spent the past three days wanting to scream, feeling like a rubber band stretched until it had to snap any minute. The bone-deep terror because somebody wanted to kill her would have been plenty on its own. But then there was Tom Moore.

Yes, she drove every day to visit Mom at the rehab facility. In theory, she could relax there. Tom discouraged any other activities, though, especially running.

"But shouldn't I be safe with you?" she'd asked. Or was that "whined"?

An expression she didn't like crossed his face.

"If he thinks the kind of attacks he's accomplished before are too high-risk, he has another option."

Jordan had instantly understood what he meant. Most of the men in town were hunters and were capable of shooting her with reasonable accuracy from a couple of blocks away, and then be on their way.

No wonder her skin crawled every time she stepped outside! Tom did believe nothing would happen daytimes—

too many potential witnesses were out and about—but why take a chance?

Sun shining outside the windows or not, Jordan hated being alone all day. She just sat waiting and listening. She lived for the moment she heard that light knock on the back door and let Tom slip in.

Depending on how late he came, they might keep a light on until a reasonable bedtime for her. After that, they'd sit together in the dark for a couple more hours. She was deeply reluctant to sleep. When she did lie down, it wasn't in her bed, but rather curled up with a mound of bedding in her closet. She'd gone upstairs, dug through the stuff she'd left here, and found her softball bat, which was now her constant companion.

Most often, in the hours she and Tom had together, they talked quietly. Favorite bands, movies, sports. Topics gradually became more personal. Tom's reminiscences weren't so much reluctant as rusty, she diagnosed, as if he had blocked a lot out for a long time. His childhood had been much tougher than hers, she quickly realized, but when she said so, he nuzzled her cheek and murmured, "Different. When I was young, I didn't expect anything else. It was tough when my foster dad died, but—"

"He died. He didn't leave you on purpose."

"Yeah," Tom said in a quiet, gravelly voice.

Jordan didn't know about him, but she'd never in her life talked to anyone as honestly. He'd reach out and take her hand; often they cuddled. Nothing in her life had ever felt as good as his solid, strong body, always warmer than hers.

He told her about the frustrations of working homicide in a large city, when separating good guys and bad guys from each other was rarely simple.

"Protecting you," he said one night, "feels clean in com-

parison with some of my investigations." He told her about
the friend who'd been killed, how much he missed him, then
about his wife and young daughter. Almost choking up,
he said, "Emilia says he'd have chosen to save me and die
himself. I think it should have been the other way around.
He had more to lose."

Jordan understood, but…she would never have met him.
She held him for a few minutes after that, although she
knew he didn't do anything like cry.

They laughed, too, also quietly. Kept dipping into shared
tastes from food to ideas for a bucket list. Sometimes she almost convinced herself they were just two people getting to
know each other—but then she'd wish desperately she could
see his face, and would remember why they sat in the dark.

And oh, she wanted him to make love with her. Every
single night, when she gave up and whispered, "Good
night," he kissed her. Those kisses grew more and more serious, deeper, hungrier, until breaking off was almost more
than she could bear. She didn't even know if he backed off
every night because of his promise to be patient—or because he really did fear he wouldn't hear a small tinkle of
glass breaking or thump that wasn't a normal night noise.

So on the fourth day, when her doorbell rang at two in
the afternoon not long after she'd gotten back from seeing
her mother, she flinched. Would she dare open the door
to *anyone*?

She did creep like a mouse to peek through the blinds.

There was Tom, holding a pizza box.

She flung open the door. "What are you *doing*?"

He grinned and stepped inside. "Visiting. Bringing you
lunch." His smile faded. "I promised I wouldn't lie to you
again. The truth is, I want to see you in daylight when we
don't have to be so on edge. But I'm also hoping that seeing us

openly socializing will make our target mad." He shrugged. "We haven't exactly been subtle about being friends and maybe more. It might have looked strange this past week, me not showing up during the day now and again."

She couldn't decide whether to laugh or cry. She'd been miserable, bored, lonely, scared, and now here he was. With pizza, no less!

"Especially now that he knows I'm a cop, he's got to be wondering what I'm doing nights," Tom told her, as they reheated the pizza in the microwave. "My best guess is that he'll believe I'm sitting at home waiting for him."

"So we want to convince him I'm also alone at night." Bait.

He didn't even try to deny that he'd set a trap with a goal of convincing this monster that Jordan was here at home, on her own and defenseless. He did give her a hard hug and say, "I'm sorry."

She smiled with difficulty. "How else can we end this?"

TOM HAD SPENT the morning doing what felt like never-ending research. His effort to find out where the killer had stayed during the week he'd potentially stalked Jordan in Walla Walla had hit a dead end. He'd searched for traffic tickets on either side of the state border. He'd prowled databases until his eyes were crossing after it occurred to him that someone who enjoyed murder might have committed the crime at other times and in places unrelated to Jordan. Nothing jumped out at him.

"That's because you're not seeing what's right in front of you," Guthrie had the nerve to say. He snorted. "That woman has you cross-tied."

Tom didn't know what his expression had given away, but the chief seemed to shrink a little and kept his mouth shut when Tom stalked out of the office. He'd been even more ticked when he'd passed Bowen lurking in the hall probably eavesdropping. The SOB had grinned.

Walking out to his vehicle, Tom decided there wasn't a reason in the world not to expose his relationship with Jordan to the world, as long as nobody had reason to think he was staying nights. It wouldn't be a bad thing if his friendliness to her served as a goad to someone angry at the idea of the police investigator potentially romancing the woman the killer hated so much.

Tom believed an attack was just a matter of time. He pictured somebody who wouldn't be able to resist, whatever the risk. Somebody driven by deep, hidden anger. Somebody who thought he was smarter than everyone else. Look how much he'd gotten away with so far. And for how long.

Because all that was true, Tom ground his teeth at the thought. Jordan had been through hell because cops had looked for the easiest answer. He wasn't letting himself off the hook.

Increasingly, he leaned toward believing the killer *wasn't* someone who vented to anyone who'd listen. Like steam, every time you let go of some of the anger, the pressure lessened. But if you let the rage eat at you, that made for an explosive buildup.

Today, eating across the table from Jordan in broad daylight, Tom stopped thinking about much of anything but how beautiful she was. How he loved seeing emotions flit across her face, the purse of her lips, the way the weight of her mass of hair emphasized the delicacy of her neck. He loved the range of her smiles, too, from impish to wistful to true happiness. He wanted to think he was responsible for that smile.

He let her talk about her mother, who was eager to come home and claimed those darned physical therapists were working her harder there than they ever had here, in her home. "She's not complaining, though. I think she's on pins and needles as much as I am."

Her mother couldn't possibly be feeling the tension Tom did, with sexual frustration twined with fear for Jordan.

He'd put the leftover pizza in the refrigerator and was leaning against the counter wondering whether he shouldn't get out of here before he did something he shouldn't, when Jordan looked at him.

"You really think we're safe right now? That he won't go for me during the day?"

"I really think," Tom agreed. Damn. Was his body betraying his thoughts?

"I...suppose you need to go?"

"I never want to go," he said, grit in his voice.

Her lips parted. "Then...would you kiss me?"

Every time she asked, it just about killed him.

"Is that all you want?" he had to ask, knowing how thin his self-restraint was.

But miracle of miracles, she shook her head. "I want you," she said softly.

He was on her so fast, she let out a startled squeak, but she also met him with open arms.

This kiss went deep and frantic within seconds. She tried to climb him, and he helped even as he tasted her, drove his tongue into her mouth, squeezed her butt and got her sweater halfway off.

Lifting his head for a breath, he took a look around. Blinds drawn and doors locked or not, the kitchen felt too open. Besides, he had to get a grip on himself. She deserved tenderness. One of his worries all along had been about what her sex life with Dunn had been like. Abusers weren't likely to be patient, gentle lovers.

But if the guy had turned her off men, it wasn't apparent now. As Tom hustled her down the short hall and into her bedroom, Jordan slid her slender hand up beneath his shirt, kneading muscles, trying to reach his belly and chest.

At her bedside, he set about stripping her with maximum speed, and her cooperation would have made it happen even faster if she hadn't also been wrestling with *his* clothes. It being winter, they were both wearing too much, in his opinion. He especially hated having to sit down to take off his boots.

But when he lifted his head, she'd just kicked off her jeans. He stared. "You're beautiful," he said hoarsely. "Perfect."

"Not compared to you." Pink-cheeked, she inspected him. He loved the way she nibbled on her lower lip.

He lunged, bore her back laughing onto the bed, and sucked her tender lip into his mouth. They kissed some more, until he couldn't wait and shifted his body lower so he could lick and suck on breasts even more gorgeous than he'd imagined. He slipped his fingers between her thighs, finding her slick and sensitive. Things sped up when she got her hand on him, squeezing and stroking until he had to roll away before this all came to an abrupt end.

His hands shook as he got the condom on. Tom didn't remember ever having that problem. He intended to slow down again as he lifted his weight over her, but her legs were splayed wide, and her arms wrapped tight around his torso. The temptation was too great. Any worry he was going too fast disappeared when she whispered, "Now," and arched her back in a spasm as he pushed inside her.

She was tight, welcoming, everything he'd ever needed. Her hips rose to meet him; she dug her fingernails into his back and came with what would have been shocking speed if he hadn't been teetering on the edge so that he fell with her. His shuddering release went on forever.

Stunned, struggling to pull air into his lungs, he could only think, *Yeah*. With Jordan, he could live gladly.

"I'VE UNDERESTIMATED THIS BASTARD," Tom growled two days later.

"You're the one who said he's not impulsive, that he's patient."

"Yeah, but—" He made a sound in his throat and pulled her close for a quick kiss. When he lifted his head, he said, "That last bit of slush melted today."

"I noticed."

Tom only nodded. The fact that it would have been next to impossible not to leave footprints was a good reason for this guy to hold off.

"I may have misjudged his intentions," he added. "He could still be zeroed in on me. If he's gotten his hands on something of yours he could plant in my house…"

With impressive calm, Jordan said, "Should we move to your house?"

"No. Then your fingerprints would be all over it." Tom sighed.

"You look awfully tired." Now she sounded tentative. He must really look haggard. "I could stay awake for a while now so you could get some sleep."

He studied her drawn face. "You're not getting much more sleep than I am."

"No, I… I suppose not."

Tom shook his head. "If he comes in shooting, you wouldn't have time to wake me up. I'll be okay." How many more nights would he be able to make that claim? If this nightmare dragged on much longer—

Quit worrying about tomorrow, he told himself. What he needed was to be sharp tonight.

Something told him when Jordan said good-night, she wouldn't be heading off to slumberland any more than he would. When that moment came, he kept the kisses gentle but unhurried. Whether she got the message he was trying to convey, he didn't know.

He did know that once he was alone in the dark, his eyelids felt as if they had ten-pound weights on them, and he had to keep getting up to walk through the house just to stay awake. Tonight, he was conscious of a level of pain he usually blanked out. No, he really didn't want to get shot again. He already felt like a damn pincushion.

Sinking back on the sofa, he listened to the silence. Jordan was in her mother's bedroom tonight. Not in the bed, in case bullets were fired right through the window.

More silence.

If I wanted to break into this house, he asked himself for the hundredth time, *how would I do it?*

JORDAN JERKED OUT of a shallow sleep threaded with nightmares.

Glass breaking had to be at the back door. By the time she understood, a distinctive *snap* told her the lock had been unengaged, and an intruder was in the kitchen.

A cry of fear escaped her before she could stifle it. She shrank deeper into the closet, shoving shoes out of the way. Tom!

Pop, pop. Those were shots, she knew, but not usual ones. A silencer? Whatever it was called. Her thoughts flew feverishly. She'd seen Tom's gun, and it wasn't fitted with anything special.

Creak. He was already right outside her bedroom door.

The next shots struck her bed, which bounced. Oh God. She tried to will herself to be part of the wall at the back of the closet. Invisible.

Except...

Pop, pop, pop. He was firing farther away now, probably into the living room. Or Mom's room. Who knew? *Please God let Tom have been awake but not have leaped out to make a target of himself.*

Then she heard his voice.

"Drop the gun!" Tom yelled. "You aren't getting away this time!"

A snarled "You're a dead man" came to her.

More shots, some louder that had to be return fire. Terrified, she knew there was nowhere in the living room for Tom to hide. What if he was gunned down? She couldn't bear it.

Jordan steeled herself to crawl out of the closet, grab her wooden bat with shaking hands, and creep toward the door.

It was like being in battle. More shots. Plaster flew, bits hitting her face. Did she dare venture into the hall? Would either man have time to change out a magazine? The killer was running out of time, Jordan realized in some remote part of her brain. Neighbors must have called 911 by now. It hadn't even occurred to her that she should have.

Bang, bang, bang. Pop, pop, pop. How could they *not* be running out of ammunition?

Suddenly there was a massive crash, and guttural, animalistic sounds. She tiptoed into the hall, wishing it wasn't so dark, but saw enough to know the two men grappled with each other, one slamming the other against the wall. One body crashed to the floor.

What if she turned on the hall light? Only...it would blind them both.

Closer, closer... Oh God, Tom was down. The man with

a knee in his belly wore something black over his head. Tom was holding on to the other man's wrists, keeping a handgun from lowering to aim at him.

Another pistol lay on the floor where she might be able to snatch it up. Only...what if Tom or this monster had discarded it because it was out of ammunition?

Whatever her vow, she'd have picked it up if she'd been sure it had bullets left. Instead, Jordan summoned rage at the man who'd used a tragedy to try to destroy her life.

She jogged the couple of steps. His head turned, but his eyes were only black holes. Now he started to wrench that gun toward her, but Tom twisted his arm, drawing it back toward himself. The killer bellowed with pain or fury, and the gun barked again. Tom's body jerked from the impact. Both brimming with adrenaline and weirdly calm, Jordan readied for her swing, just as if she stood at home plate, and took it with everything in her.

The impact was hideous, like shattering a pumpkin, but she didn't care. She let the bat drop with a clatter, turned on the light, and fell to her knees beside Tom...and the man who lay unmoving, sprawled half atop him.

TOM HEARD HIMSELF swearing as he shoved the SOB off, rolled, tried to sit up. "Jordan—"

"Did I kill him?" She sounded...he couldn't decide.

"I don't know." Damn, he hurt. Yeah, he'd been shot again despite believing he was prepared. Would he have won the battle for the gun in his assailant's hands if Jordan hadn't intervened? He couldn't be sure and could never regret taking a bullet meant for Jordan.

"Sweetheart," he managed to say. "Come here."

Sirens were so close, he didn't know how he'd missed hearing them approaching.

"I have to let them in." Her voice was high, but she was hanging in there.

"Yeah. Okay."

He'd recognized the voice and not been surprised. He'd just as soon Uncle Ronnie was dead, but for Jordan's sake, it might be better if the bastard survived to be convicted to a lifetime in the penitentiary—the sentence he'd wanted *her* to serve. He could think about her every day for the rest of his life.

Tom couldn't quite make himself try to stand up.

Within seconds, they were swarmed with cops and medics.

"Take some photos before you move either of us," he snapped. Damn, was that Bussert looking so shocked?

From then on, events passed like a series of slides. As they loaded him to take him to the hospital, he heard Jordan again asking if Bowen was dead. Saying, "I hit him. He was trying to kill us both."

Then she saw that they were hustling Tom out, and tried to follow. When she got close enough to grab his hand, he tried to squeeze hers but failed. "S'okay," he said. "They need to ask questions."

"I'm sorry! So sorry!" Tears ran down her face, now that it was over. That's the picture he carried until, damn, he was under a bright light and a woman with a mask covering her face threatened to knock him out again. His last thought was comforting: this time, he believed Jordan would be waiting for him when he woke up.

Epilogue

Jordan had never envisioned the fallout beyond her small circle.

At first, once Tom recovered consciousness, she was occupied squelching his determination to beat himself up. He hadn't been asleep when Bowen broke in, but had been a step too slow. He should have rebounded faster from his previous injuries. Were all men like that? Jordan wondered.

She'd silenced him by insisting he was her hero, although he was determined to deny that. *She'd* saved him.

"I wish you could have seen yourself," he said. "Warrior woman. Although I hope I never see that expression on your face again."

She'd been trying to convince him he didn't have to pretend he didn't hurt, but in truth, his surgeon had encouraged him to get up and move. So now she and he were walking the hospital corridor just as she'd done with her mother a few months ago. He wore a sling, the bullet having struck the same shoulder as the previous wound. The surgeon had an air of reserve talking about what he'd done that made Jordan wonder how much of a mess it was in there.

Now, pausing at a rare window to look outside, Tom told her that ballistics had already established that Ronald Bowen had used the same gun to shoot Elliott and kill Colin Parnell—as well as wound Tom *twice*. They had him cold…if he lived. Bowen hadn't yet regained consciousness. Jordan didn't feel as squeamish about that as she would have expected to.

Tom also told her that the mayor had stopped to speak to him that morning while she'd been meeting a contractor who would have to erase evidence of the gun battle in Mom's house before Jordan could bring her home. She'd rather her mother not see the torn plaster and wood, bullet holes in the front window and blood staining the floors.

"Guthrie has resigned. I don't know if it was under pressure or not." Tom's voice hardened. "If he hadn't, I'd have pushed for it."

"But…why?"

"He had to know about Bowen's relationship with Steve. It was bad enough that he let Steve's uncle investigate you, given his partiality, but he should have understood that Bowen was a potential suspect in the murders. He either didn't, which is inexcusable, or he did and was complicit in two murders and several attempted murders." Tom shrugged his good shoulder. "Either way, he had to go."

"So why you?" she asked, although she had a suspicion.

"He wants me to take over the department. No one else is remotely qualified."

Since they had reached his hospital room again, which fortunately he had to himself, she waited until he had laboriously stretched out in bed again, stifling only a few groans, before asking, "What did you say?"

"I agreed on an interim basis." He watched her with familiar intentness. She basked in the rich blue of his eyes.

When he tugged, she sat on the bed. She didn't remove her hand from his warm clasp.

"Do you *want* to be police chief?"

"Right now, yes. This department needs a major house-

cleaning. Officers are inadequately trained, haven't been
reined in the way they should be." He grimaced. "After
that… I don't know. I think it's realistic to guess I've been
shot a few too many times to ever plan to go back to an active job."

She wished she could tell how he felt about that. He had
to regret not being able to pack up and return to San Francisco, didn't he?

Was he trying to read her, too? She wished she had as
much confidence as she'd like, but did feel as if she had
bubbles in her bloodstream. That had to be hope, didn't it?
After the way he'd touched her, held her, the driving urgency of his lovemaking, she wanted so much to believe
he could be falling in love with her.

When she stayed silent, he continued haltingly, "This
is really soon, but as far as I'm concerned, where I work
has to do with you."

The beat of her heart quickened.

"As long as you're here for your mother, as long as you
want me around, I'll stay. But once your mother doesn't need
you on an everyday basis, if you decide to go back to school
to finish your BA or to grad school, I can get a job wher-
ever we go."

We. He couldn't have used a more powerful word. No,
he hadn't said, *I love you*. Anyone with sense would say it
was too soon. Except Jordan knew that as far as she was
concerned, it wasn't.

He was holding himself very still, she realized. He wasn't
sure of her.

She swallowed. "I would…really like that."

His breath came out ragged. "Do you remember what I
told you about my friend Max's wife?"

Jordan nodded, feeling a painful swell of pity for a woman

who'd lost the man she loved in exactly the way Jordan had just almost lost Tom.

"She knew about my background. That I'd become used to being alone. She all but whacked me over the head and insisted that, thanks to Max, I'd been given a chance to have everything. A wife, children, happiness. I mostly put what she said out of my mind until I met you. It was like a door opening, except after all my lies, I could see you closing and locking it. I couldn't imagine you forgiving me."

His raw, emotional admission brought the sting of tears to her eyes. With a cry, she bent forward to press her cheek against his, prickly from lack of shaving. She didn't dare hug him. He had to hurt everywhere.

"You were wrong," she whispered. "Of course I forgave you. And…and I want children and happiness, too. With you."

Tom's one good arm closed around her tightly enough to suggest he didn't intend to ever let her go, and she smiled and cried both. How had events so terrible led to this kind of joy?

* * * * *

HARLEQUIN
Reader Service

Enjoyed your book?

Try the perfect subscription for Romance readers and get more great books like this delivered right to your door.

See why over 10+ million readers have tried Harlequin Reader Service.

Start with a Free Welcome Collection with free books and a gift—valued over $20.

Choose any series in print or ebook.
See website for details and order today:

TryReaderService.com/subscriptions